SCENT
of a Lion

by Lindsay McAuley

Published in Australia in 2024 by Lindsay McAuley
Email: Linzi7272@gmail.com
Website: lindsaymcauley.com

© Lindsay McAuley 2024

The moral right of the author has been asserted.

ISBN 9780646898407 (Paperback)

A catalogue record of this book is available from the National Library of Australia.

Disclaimer:
The author has made every attempt to ensure the accuracy of the information in this book was correct at the time of publication. The author does not assume and hereby disclaims any liability to any party for any loss, damage or disruption caused by errors or omissions, whether such errors or omissions result from accident, negligence, or any other cause.

Cover design by Lindsay McAuley
Graffic art by Deitmar Kuhn
Epilogue photo by Lindsay McAuley
Author photo by Linda Higgs-Weitzel

Typeset in Garamond Premier Pro 11pt

For all wanderers, who move to rest.

With special thanks to Ken, Linda, Wendy, and Lucy
who helped make this book a reality.

Calum is spending the evening inside on a couch, soft and comforting, a cat, curled up beside him. A fireplace, burns bright, its glow, bringing ambiance to the room as snow falls outside. The autumn colours, so beautiful, are surrendering to a monotone, handsome and cold. Molly purrs.

"Winter is here at last," he sighs. "At last."

The movie he is watching, is coming to an end. The conflict of the story, about to be resolved.

"You were just a kitten when we first saw this movie so long ago. Now look at us."

He has seen this drama several times. Each time, he feels disappointed. It doesn't have the resolution he wants.

They need to be together from the moment they both fell in love, he thought. From that time on, until forever. Would she ever understand that?

That is how Calum thought a true romance movie should end. They never end.

Chapter One

The subway train slows as it nears Gangdong station in Seoul, South Korea. Calum and Halla are on their way back to their suburb, having been to lunch across the Han River. They are both in a jovial, playful mood.

"There is a seat available over there for the elderly," said Halla, hoping to provoke a response. "It's empty. Would you like to sit down?"

"Oh sure, but ladies first. This one is for women who are pregnant. Come, let me help you," replied Calum.

Calum began urging Halla to a seat. The other passengers show little interest in sharing their humour, avoiding eye contact, intent on their own business.

"Be careful with our baby," said Calum.

It had been a wonderful day, making jokes, playing together like adolescent teenagers. They have known each other only a week, meeting on Calum's second day in Seoul, after arriving from Australia. Their love is new. They are experiencing the happiness of being in each other's company, in fact, they have difficulty being away from one another.

For Halla, their romance has brought mental conflict. This is her first love affair after many years of abstinence. Although having made a determined choice not to complicate her life by being in a relationship, this sudden connection has a resonance that runs deep. She is concerned that within the lure of fulfilment, their journey may also hold the peril of heartbreak. Calum cannot believe his luck, having a beautiful Korean lady to accompany him on his travels.

The joy of the day is about to change for them. It starts with what sounds like sirens. Numerous mobile phones make a piercing, screaming noise.

With a horrified look, Halla peers at her phone. Calum is not comprehending what is the cause, his phone needs charging. Looking at her and at the expressions of other people, it is obvious something is seriously wrong, their faces white with fear.

"We have to get off urgently," said Halla. She pulls him close, moving toward the door of the carriage. "I will explain soon."

The other passengers are off their seats in a second, also making a rush to the exit.

"What's happening?" said Calum, completely baffled. He is surprised to see Koreans being so assertive. Usually, they are polite and considerate, yet now, they are jostling for position as though their lives depend on it. As the train brakes, the squealing wheels add another discordant sound to the crescendo.

"Stay with me," she said, "We will be out soon."

They are pressed up against the exit doors by the rest of the passengers, some anxiously trying to call relatives. Calum cannot understand a word of what is being said or the reason for the commotion, his feeling of unease escalates, both by the dramatic change in the mood of the environment and his own ignorance of the situation. Halla's eyes tell the story, one of stark fear, but why, and why so suddenly?

The doors open, the ominous sound of public sirens echo

throughout the train station. The intensity, deafening and menacing, fill every nook and cranny within the confined spaces of the subway platforms. A great weight of uncertainty is upon Calum. He doesn't want to die today, in a subway in South Korea, or anywhere else for that matter.

It is comforting to know he has Halla with him to interpret, but she isn't letting him in on the details of the unfolding crisis. "Come this way," she says, tugging at his arm. "Move quickly!" she added, intent on keeping the reason for the drama secret, so as not to cause Calum additional alarm. They are squeezed up against a cold tiled wall by the anxious crowd.

"Halla! What is going on? Is a volcano erupting?"

"No, worse."

He wonders what could be more devastating than a volcano spewing ash everywhere.

"It's a Presidential Alert. We must stay down here in the subway. It is safer. We cannot go up the stairs," her voice fragile and fearful.

The event sharpens Halla's reaction in ways she is unaccustomed, the catalyst orchestrating a combination of physiological and mental responses. As the possibility of death seizes her, an intense yearning for a safe refuge propels her to act. The flight/flight response to fear surges through her veins, a torrent of vitality coursing within.

This intricate drama begins within the sanctuary of her amygdala, a part of the brain which processes emotions. Her breathing quickens. Her heart rate increases with an elevation of blood pressure. Peripheral blood vessels constrict, as the central vessels around vital organs dilate, flooding with oxygen and nutrients. Feeling unusually strong, muscles are pumped with blood, even those at the base of each hair follicle, becoming tighter, causing piloerection. The levels of glucose spike producing an unfamiliar store of energy. Calcium and white cells increase. Electrical signals from the hypothalamus to the pituitary gland begin communicating. Her body responds with a sudden urge of diarrhea. She is hard wired to escape.

Then, a few seconds later, another barrage of alerts come across millions of mobile phones simultaneously.

"What is it this time?" said Calum, his heart rate, loud enough to be audible.

"A false alarm. They made an error," replied Halla.

The public sirens become silent, as abruptly as they started.

"They made an error? About what?" said Calum.

"Our Government sent a message. A rocket left North Korea and was headed this way, but it broke apart," she explained.

"That's serious. A missile headed this way?"

"It was a satellite launch. The Chollima-1. But our government sent an alert anyway, by mistake. I thought it was all over for us for a moment." she added.

"Unbelievable!" replied Calum.

"Everything ok now," she said, trying to convince herself as well.

"That's serious. I suppose it is better to be a false alarm than not making any mention at all," he replied.

Even with the relief of a false alarm, Halla is still showing an extreme level of anxiety. She wants to get out of there, back home to the familiarity of her surroundings and especially, her pets. They will be sensing her worry and concern from afar. The effect of her mental state, reflected visibly as beads of sweat roll down her face. The experience is similar to a near death experience for her, as for millions of other people.

Yet, amidst this bodily tumult, an unforeseen desire stirs, a mysterious undercurrent that defies the logic of her immediate predicament. The urge to succumb to the magnetic pull of passion becomes an overwhelming force. She wants to rip Calum's clothes off and make mad passionate love right there in the subway, regardless of who is watching. In the concealed recesses of her subconscious, this powerful longing for sensual embrace surfaces. As if ensnared by a spell, a forbidden fantasy unfolds in her mind, the rising tide of sexual desire eclipsing the madness evolving around her. She desires a tempestuous liaison, a union of souls, born out of the bustling chaos of fear.

"I no feel good, I must go now. Wait for me at your hotel. I will contact," said Halla, as she vanishes into the crowd.

The urgency of escape intertwined with the seductive call of sexual surrender, leaves her emotionally torn apart. She resists the temptation, slipping up the steps into daylight as though emerging from the primal darkness of death, carrying the residue of a tumultuous journey etched forever upon her soul. She feels the conflict between the urgency of escape and the intoxicating allure of a socially unacceptable embrace. It is the phenomena called, end-of-the-world sex that is enveloping her.

Now, she needs to find a toilet urgently.

What was once totally inconceivable to become a victim of nuclear destruction, becomes very real for Calum. Never before has the spectre of death been so close. This is usually the subject of historical movies, television scenes of Hiroshima, far removed from personal reality. It is the first time in his life he has to consider the end, as it is for millions of other people. Images from World War 2 in Japan, showing burnt victims in tattered clothing flicker through his mind. He wonders if humanity has any real hope for the future, unable to understand how anyone can find joy in the suffering of others. Jostled along with the crowd moving up the stairs into the daylight, the experience, a precious reminder of the fragile circumstances in balance that shields his mortality.

Halla is nowhere to be seen. A nearby cafe provides a quick boost for his mobile phone.

Calum: Are you ok? Tell me when you get to your place.

While residents of Seoul are used to living in the shadow of threats from their nuclear-armed neighbour, an element of complacency is creeping in among many people about the risks and how to respond. False alarms are contributing to a sense of apathy. Yet, today is a stark reminder of the precious value the lives of their loved ones are to them.

When Halla returns to her unit she holds her dog, Mongee, telling her how much she is loved and not chastising her for making the now predictable mess on the bed. Songee, her cat, is also lavished with more affection than usual. Finally, Calum returns to her consciousness. She sends him a text.

Halla: I am scared of you. You dangerous kangaroo.
Calum: It wasn't my fault.
Halla: I want peaceful life. Not same you. Not need men.
Calum: It would have happened with or without me being with you.

Calum feels he is copping the brunt of North Korea's actions.

Calum: I would come over to comfort you but you won't give me your address. You know where I am. The door is open for you.

Halla is too angry and upset to cry. Yet, in her mental anguish, there is a rising sense of vulnerability, a need to be comforted, to be connected.

Halla: I am home. I come soon.

Chapter Two

The rebellion of Halla's physical desires is destroying her fortress of self-reliance, leaving her disoriented, a reality that contradicts the principles she clings to so fiercely. Berating herself for succumbing to the lure of seduction, she had sworn off the need for men, yet Calum, with his magnetic presence and allure, is becoming the instrument shattering her resolve. She is now a wreckage of her own making, confusion, a guilty partner in her demise.

Yet in her heart, the call to be with him is stronger than the isolation she once saw as her unshakeable future. She believes the universe has spoken to her and the message obvious, though not without an extreme personal challenge. She vacillates, then a decision becomes clear, for now.

"All or nothing!" she said.

Inside Halla's unit, she has a sacred space prepared. In times of stress and anxiety, it is to this safe refuge she retreats, in search of solace. Upon entering, she bows to show humility, a practice born of ancient tradition. On the wall, above her mother's ornate table made from the wood of the Ginkgo tree, hangs a painting she had done of 'Jacheongbi', the Korean Goddess of love. Inside the table is hidden the name of her deity on white paper, hand written in red ink. Littered around are numerous offering bowls and incense pots. There are some old coins in disarray, along with coloured stones, small pieces of hemp clothing and earthen jars filled with grain. Ambient light filters through a coloured stained-glass window, through which a blurred image of a bridge over a river can be seen.

The flickering flames from three black candles cast shadows on an ancient book she is about to consult. Opening the well-worn pages of the weathered text, it holds atavistic secrets of enchantment, passed down through generations. Halla turns through several formulas, *'Eternal Youth', 'Wealth and Fortune'*, stopping on a page entitled, *'Initiation'*.

Her eyes sparkle with a new sense of hope and fervour, having decided to prepare a love potion for Calum.

She carefully arranges an array of containers, each holding an assortment of herbs and spices. Into a crystal glass, she delicately measures out portions of Horney Goat weed, its properties known to kindle passion. Next comes Sichuan peppercorn, a spice that adds another potent fire of pheromones and lust to her concoction.

As a little girl, her Grand Mother had given her a mortar and pestle. Brought to Korea during the Mongol invasion during the mid 13th century, it is therefore over 700 years old and one of Halla's most prized possessions. Now, it is in the hands of a woman embarking on a quest for love.

She grinds the ingredients into a fine powder, each twist of the pestle, a step that connects her to the process of magic.

In the midst of this arcane ritual, two dolls are placed at the centre of a triangle formed by a careful arrangement of the candles. One doll, adorned in Korean traditional dress, the other, wearing only a hat and belt. They symbolize a connection that transcends time and tradition. Silk threads intertwine the dolls, binding them in a symbolic union. The dolls are sprinkled with Calum's short strands of hair retrieved from his accommodation earlier. With a sense of accomplishment, Halla begins her incantation.

"Warm seed, love run strong; warm heart, let us never part," she chants, her voice merging with the fragrance of the herbs and the flickering candlelight.

With ceremonial reverence, Halla adds the finely ground powder to a crystal decanter containing a traditional light-pink liqueur, Gamhongno, an elixir made with medicinal herbs. To this, a mixture of hallucinogenic fermented mushrooms is blended. As the ingredients dissolve, she swears a proclamation to the universe; "I will make him love me. He must follow the script," her words charged with unwavering certainty. The final signature, to pour hot candle wax over silk threads binding the dolls. The ceremony is sealed. The concoction now ready.

Trusting in the magic she has woven to bind them for all time, she makes her way to an unsuspecting Calum, the vessel of love carefully wrapped in cloth nestled safely in the console of her car. She needs reassurance, human contact. Above all else, a hug, to help remove the intensity of the day.

"Why you no lock door? It's not safe," said Halla, upon entering Calum's hotel room.

Quickly grabbing the sheets to cover his exposed body, Calum replied. "So you could get in of course. I might have gone to sleep." Calum pats the bed indicating to Halla she could sit down. "Come."

"I brought you something, a herbal liqueur to help you sleep. Drink," she commands.

"You are so kind, always thinking of me" replied Calum, as he sips the potion. "Do you have some for yourself?"

"It's for you, my kangaroo. I use bathroom," she said, as she departs.

"That outfit looks so interesting. I love the hat," Calum compliments. "You look different every time I see you," he added.

"Thank you. Gamsahamnida." replied Halla, not revealing her clothes are out of necessity, one of her many public disguises.

In the mirror, the first thing Halla notices is a blemish on her cheek. Calum might have seen it already. She curses. She takes a long look at herself, realising she has let herself enter a hotel room where there is a man lying on the bed waiting for her. Anything can happen from this moment on. She considers the aftermath of a sexual encounter, the possibility of pregnancy and therefore, a lifetime of sacrifice rearing children. But a fire is burning deep inside her and there is someone near who can stoke her embers. It is Calum she wants, but more than that, she needs to feel safe and protected and he has made himself available.

"Miss Halla, where are you?" Calum calls, in a playful mood. "I am waiting for you." Under his breath he murmurs. "Don't keep a hungry lion waiting."

Halla enters the room to see Calum's arms outstretched. He smiles at her as she sits on the end of the bed, a short distance from him. As much as she cannot wait to be immersed in his arms, she plays the cautious, semi-interested role.

"You like?" said Halla, pointing at the empty glass of liqueur.

"It has an unusual taste. What's in it?" he replied.

"Magic," she said, refusing to reveal its true intent and purpose.

She studies him looking for signs of the effect of her love potion. His eyes shine more intensely than before, a blue that makes the depths of the ocean look pale.

Halla is fully clothed and Calum dressed only in a pair of shorts, his bare chest and upper arms alluring. With her heart full of expectation, she moves closer, the pillow softening under her weight. It wraps around her as she lies on her back, waiting expectedly. "I am here," she whispers.

"We have had a big day, you and me," said Calum.

"Yes, a big day, I will never forget," replied Halla, staring at the ceiling, tears forming in her eyes. "But I want to forget. I wish the North Korean president would die."

"Forget about North Korea. It's over now and I am so glad you are here with me," said Calum, as he stretches his arm across to hold her body, accidently bumping her breasts in the process. He is surprised she allows him to rub across them without resistance. "You're safe here Halla. We survived and lived to tell the tale. That is all that matters."

"I was so scared. I thought it was the end, the end of me, of us... everything."

In an effort to provide comfort, Calum spoke. "Me too. I have never experienced anything like it," his fingers gently tracing the contours and curves of her skin. Halla awaits the moment when destiny and desire converge and her potion works its magic.

Surprised by his own assertiveness, his hand slips under her top edging gently towards the upper part of her bra cup. Still no resistance, but more than that, Halla guides his hand a little closer. She gives him secret permission to push further. Now he is underneath her bra where he finds her soft warm breasts. He glides his hands across from one to the other, squeezing her small hard nipples between his fingers. Halla breathes heavily, her back arching, raising her breasts higher to meet the firm roughness of Calum's strong hands.

"I love you, Calum. I don't like you. I love you." She surprises herself with her humour, considering the unfamiliarity of her circumstances.

It's been years since a man has fondled her breasts. An electrifying sensation is travelling to all parts of her body, down her arms, her legs, but especially across her inner thighs, upwards to her vagina causing a warm, receptive moistening. Above her, the fan spins slowly, mirroring the swirling motions of the conflict in her mind as her body responds to his touch. She is becoming ready to receive, her legs parting, her nipples erect. Touch is what she wants, what she needs, now more than ever.

Calum whispers in her ear. "Feel, don't think. If you want me to stop, just say stop."

Halla's mind drifts to her fantasy realm momentarily. She remembers that comment was in her dreamscape, but now is a time to be in the present. "Feel, don't think," said Halla, as she slips her hand under the elastic of his shorts, not all the way, just enough to tantalise and tease.

"Let's take these off," said Calum, as he tugs at her bra and top. She responds by rolling on her side allowing access to the connections. As her bra falls away, the buttons on her top surrender, she is now fully exposed. Self-conscious, her hands unsuccessfully covering her breasts, yet she loves the excitement, the unrealised potential of the moment. What will he do to her next? she wonders.

"Relax my mystery lady, just let it happen and enjoy," he said, as he coaches her hands away leaving her upright breasts fully exposed and aching for touch.

As his lips gently surround her nipples, she makes soft, seductive sounds. Then, her hand falls back slipping past the elastic of his shorts. Now she has his manhood in her hand. "A monster," she purrs, as her stroking motion makes him throb harder and her, wetter than ever.

He pulls at the elastic of her underpants letting go, causing a slapping sound as it meets her skin. She knows what he is implying, raising her bottom so her underwear can glide off easily. They slip away. The last wall of resistance, gone.

Both Calum and Halla are a blank canvas of desire and want, ready to be painted with the hues of passion. They find themselves on the precipice of an intimate moment. Stripped bare of all inhibitions, their bodies lay exposed, vulnerable, yet empowered, and the air crackles with anticipation.

In that sacred space, time slows, an acknowledgment of the profound connection unfolding. The room echoes with whispered promises and exchanged glances, seductive sounds and low murmurs, as they embark on a maiden voyage into the realm of love making. The outside world fades away, leaving only the raw authenticity of two souls on the precipice of an all-encompassing connection, written in the poetic language of the night.

Her legs widen further making her yearning crevice accessible, aching, soft and moist, but most of all, inviting. Calum's hand makes its way across her soft, smooth skin to the inside of her thighs-so near, so close. She feels it, the entry of his prying fingers, gliding in and out slowly and rhythmically. Oh, it feels so, so good. She can sense it rise up from inside her, the unstoppable pent-up pleasure about to find release.

And it does. Calum feels her hand grip his member like a vice. If she squeezes any harder, he is worried the end will fly off and hit the ceiling, like a cork leaving a champagne bottle. She is reaching climax. It is coming together, the joy and pleasure sweeping over her like a fresh warm wind. She succumbs as never before and then, falls back spent from the physical release. The sensations and emotion overwhelm her. She turns on to her side away from Calum, softly sobbing.

"Are you ok?" said Calum.

Suddenly conscious of her modesty, Halla ejects from the bed as one would fly from a trampoline. Scrambling urgently for her clothes scattered among the bedraggled sheeting, she avoids eye contact. "I not need. Not want men." She puts on her clothes and exits the hotel room.

Calum mumbles to himself. "I should not have done that. "Halla! Wait! Where are you going?" He scrambles for his clothes.

Halla has her car started by the time Calum catches up with her in the car park. "Halla, what's wrong? I am sorry," he pleads.

"I go home. I cannot keep up with the kangaroo. This too hard. You have many girlfriends before. I know." Her car screeches away into the night leaving Calum in disbelief.

Halla doesn't make it home. A storm rages in her heart, compelling her to stop her car to collect her thoughts. Heavy with the scent of regret and confusion, she finds herself sitting in solitude, waiting to untangle the knots of the diverse feelings that bind the emotional tempest churning within. Anger, her familiar, yet uninvited guest, has settled again in the corners of her mind. It is the violation of her cardinal rule which confronts her—to stand untethered, unbridled by the complexities of entangled affections. Independence had been her ally, shielding her from the pitfalls of emotional hurt. But now, in the aftermath of this encounter with Calum, she finds herself standing on the precipice of vulnerability. The carefully constructed wall she has built around her heart, is crumbling.

Calum: Halla. I am so sorry.

Amidst the echoes of her anger and self-reproach, an unsettling truth challenges her—a profound sense of incompleteness. The yearning refuses to be silenced. Denial is a fragile shield. This fleeting encounter has only scratched the surface, the journey into passion just beginning. The road ahead, beckons her and repels her to confront the complexities of self-discovery, a winding path, a minefield, promising both peril and adoration. She knows the universe has called them together, but can she fulfill its demands and expectations?

Halla: I need time.

Calum shares Halla's confusion, but in a different way. His self-reproach comes from the uncertainty that perhaps he took advantage of her. Did he move too fast? he wonders. Maybe she isn't ready to engage in pleasures of the flesh. For him, the passion is all encompassing. The seduction, obviously too much for her, yet he senses her urge to be touched and fondled. Like a cat on heat, he could feel her mood, purring sometimes, then hissing the next, a merry-go round of conflicting emotions. "Women!" Calum's head spun, trying to resolve the mystery of the female of his species.

Halla: I hate you.

Calum: Do you love me more than you hate me

The level of sexual energy in the hotel room, was more than Halla had anticipated, realising her love potion is only just beginning to take effect on him. Anxiety washes over her, for she knows the night is yet to bring challenges he has never experienced and their relationship, about to change forever. There is a long silence before the next text arrives from her. But when it comes, Calum finds relief, finally able to feel some peace from what could easily be described as a day from hell.

Halla: Yes. I love you more.

She has become an enigma to him, amazed how life has changed in the short time since meeting her. As he wanders back in time, he can see Halla walking out of a dream into his life. The soft breeze against his skin, the blue/green river and the overhanging Ginkgo trees decorating the shoreline, all so real in his mind's eye. He holds the vision close, as the recollection becomes increasingly vivid. The love potion courses through his veins, caressing his imagination, in readiness to unleash immense transformative power on its unwitting victim.

As sleep envelops him, the last image in his mind, is of the very first time he saw her.

Chapter Three

The most striking thing is its unremarkable qualities, the predictable orientation and the design, replicated a million times over. Unimaginative, a prominent characteristic. For some, it's an annoying object in the foreground of a picturesque cityscape, serving no other purpose than to allow a momentary respite. Yet for Calum, the park bench where he sits, provides a fortuitous opportunity, more by chance than intention.

Halla is out for a morning walk, her pace measured by a dog, whose vigour has been stolen by the absence of youth. Halla and Calum notice each other briefly as the pathway leads directly past him, ending a short distance further on. She is compelled to retrace her footsteps.

Calum knew there is risk involved. The next few moments could mean total rejection, or the start of a whole new adventure. He considers the possibility of dismissal briefly, deciding instead, to take the opportunity to intercept her on her return.

Then it began. Events unfold, that will change their lives forever.

"That's a nice-looking little dog you have," said Calum, hoping to disguise his true opinion of dogs with a compliment.

Dogs are not his favourite animal. He tolerates them, but prefers cats, appreciating their soft flexibility, the purring sounds they make stretched out beside a warm fire on a cold winter's night. He compares them to some playful women he has known as a younger man; how they crave to be desired, their willingness to surrender themselves to touch, to be rubbed and stroked. Calum loves the feminine allure of the feline species.

"Thank you. Her name is Mongee," Halla replied.

Their eyes meet briefly during this casual interchange, holding gaze a little longer than usual. Halla is assessing the things most women do when alone to ensure their safety, her antenna raised, scanning for signs of possible danger. She calculates his age, what he is wearing, his demeanour and of course, the colour of his eyes.

Calum has forgotten the dog's name already as the small animal waddled its way to his feet. He knows an assessment is underway. Halla is reassured. If Mongee is comfortable with a stranger, that is a good sign. Her faithful friend will warn her if there is a threat to her personal safety. She isn't scurrying away at his touch. Dogs know. They are sensitive, Halla thought to herself.

"She is a Pomeranian," Halla added.

"Nice," Calum replied. "I like her."

As he strokes the short strands of matted hair on the back of the aging canine, Calum knows he has crossed a major hurdle. Mongee becomes the silent arbiter of trust, easing Halla's cautious heart. He looks up, noticing shiny strands of hair gently flicker across Halla's dark intelligent eyes. The morning sun caresses her oval face, revealing a kind gentle soul, he thought. She is slight of form and attractive, close to his own height. In the background, the Han River weaves its way through the city of Seoul. All probability suggests she is a local, confirmed by the faltering English and the obvious Asian appearance.

"Beautiful day," Halla said, her flawed pronunciation, filling a momentary pause in dialogue.

The scanning continues. He is obviously a foreigner, a traveller. But what country? In his late forties, reasonably fit with a rugged handsome face. She is intrigued, yet holding herself back so as not to show too much interest. She gives a gentle tug on the lease. Mongee returns obediently to her owner.

"Yes, beautiful," he replied. "Such a beautiful river," he added, extending the preamble for as long as possible. "So many bridges. Tell me, what is it called?"

"That bridge you mean?" said Halla. His unassuming question strikes a chord with her. It means the birth of something exquisitely profound. In that instant, a mysterious scenario begins evolving in her creative mind.

"Well, yes, the river, what is it called? And that bridge, what is the name of it?" he said, prolonging the conversation until it comes time to ask the question.

"It's the Han River," she replied. "And that is the Grand Olympic bridge. It's very photographic isn't it. The Grand Olympic bridge over the Grand Han River," Halla adds for amusement.

"It sure is," he replied.

He cannot judge the effect this entire introductory, somewhat trivial conversation is having on her. She conceals her thought processes well. To him, the bridge, albeit impressive, is just a means for traffic to transverse the water. He is more preoccupied by her beauty, framed by the cerulean colour of the river. The lush green foliage lining the river banks compliments her light green shorts. Her white cotton top, shimmering in the sunlight, is set against the towering silver skyscrapers dominating the skyline. She completes a truly picturesque scene reminding Calum he is in a foreign land, only a short distance from the demilitarised zone separating it from its neighbour, North Korea.

For Halla, the bridge is far more symbolic. It is a metaphor connecting two opposite forces, the imaginary, illusionary world of dreams which she prefers, with that of the mundane existence of the physical plane. She hides her disbelief he asked about the bridge, as his question is the catalyst for her to consider the profound synchronicity of their chance meeting.

It is here, in the September autumn on an unassuming park bench, beside a river near a bridge, on Calum's second day in the country that a fire is ignited, for both of them. Such different thoughts are running through their minds simultaneously, it is surprising they are able to engage in conversation at all. She is in the process of looking for signs, more validation that this scene is creating a reality she envisions in her fanciful dreams. He is oblivious to how she paints the event in her mind, still trying to negotiate how he might pose the question that he has wanted to ask since first seeing her.

Then he feels it rise up from deep within him, the question, forming almost automatically. The words want to escape the prison of his mind, regardless of the damage that may occur as a result of their liberation. They do, finding a release during a small pause in conversation.

"Can I buy you a coffee?" he said, elevating the last word to emphasise it is a question.

There, it is out; the question. He is thankful the words formed in a comprehendible order. Now there is the eternity of suspense, the long wait for the reply; the silent void, empty, yet full of unpredictability and potential. Be prepared, he thought. Did he time it right? Anything can happen from this moment on.

However, it is caution that influences Halla's response. "I think about," she said. With that, she musters her struggling pet up to her breast and continues on her way, not waiting for him to reply. She feels it necessary to take the opportunity to depart in order to consider the invitation.

"Ok sure, I understand," Calum said, finding a suitable tone to subdue his feeling of rejection.

It was a long shot. It failed.

As Halla walks away, she retrieves a vanity mirror from her handbag. It is a ploy designed to see behind her and to know if he is still seated. Let him wait, she said to herself steeling a glance back when certain he isn't looking. She keeps walking. Mongee looks over her shoulder knowing intuitively, that it will not be the last time she would see him.

He photographs the river with the Olympic bridge in the background, noticing its magnificent steel framework and support cables, an outstanding display of engineering and artistic achievement. He remains near the park bench until she is out of sight. That's that, he thought to himself. Nothing ventured, nothing gained. He brushes his hands across some nearby grass in an effort to remove the smell of her dog from his presence. Then begins the walk back to his accommodation.

Halla notices Calum photograph the bridge. To anyone else, it would have meant nothing. To her, it is astounding, like a fantasy being replayed in reality from her favourite movie genre, romance. A spark is ignited, causing her to ponder the implications deeply. She has walked this way many times in her lifetime, but today something changed. Time and fate conspired for both their paths to intersect. She feels unusual and questions the encounter. This one is different, she muses. Is he the one who has come through the veil, finally to be with her? A sense of urgency moves her on. Mongee is surprised by the sudden shift of her impatient tread.

Who was I, passed this way?

Who now, passes here?

The answer hangs suspended.

Far enough away to remain out of sight, this event is watched from within the shadows of the overhanging branches of a Ginkgo tree. A suspicious gaze, observed this casual meeting. In his mind is conceived numerous scenarios which provokes as many unanswered questions. Why make contact here, in this relatively quiet area of Seoul, rarely visited by foreigners? What secret messages are exchanged? Intrigue swells within his imagination along with a determination to resolve the mystery. He sends a text.

I have found her!

Chapter Four

There are numerous restaurants on the footpath towards Calum's hotel and their menu is rarely printed in English. He wonders what he will find to eat on his three-week stay in the country. The geometric style of the characters of the Korean text fascinates him, the native alphabet of which is called, Hangul. He learns it was created single-handedly by King Sejong in the mid fifteenth century. Calum thought to himself, how interesting, the capacity for just one person to change the world. Now, if he could only change his own.

After his latest unsuccessful attempt at securing a date and a twenty-year marriage ending just two years earlier, he suspects the prospect of true companionship is an unrealistic dream. Thoughts of romance are often accompanied with jaded expectations. At forty-five and set in his ways, he believes that finding a partner is increasingly unlikely. As he wonders if he should revise his opening line to something more original, a car slows down beside him. The horn toots. To his amazement, it's her. Halla motions him to get into the passenger seat.

"Coffee?" Halla askes, as she re-enters the stream of traffic.

"Let's do that," Calum replied. "I know a place nearby, but I'm not sure if I can find it."

"It's ok. I know a place...we go there. We drive."

Calum is taken by surprise. How is this happening? he wonders, and where is the dog? Once out of sight, she must have raced home, deposited it somewhere, hurriedly got in her car with the intention of catching up with him. Suddenly, she is less than a meter away and they are driving away together.

Halla can only partially concentrate on driving. Now she has the opportunity to get a closer look at Calum. Dressed in blue jean shorts and a white t-shirt under a denim shirt, his hat looks as though it needs a good wash. The boots he wears are designed for hiking, not something someone would wear around the streets of Seoul. He gives off an unpleasant, sweaty odor as a result of the September humidity. Yet, it is somehow manly, wild and scruffy. Firemen and lumberjacks would probably smell like this. There is a tinge of burnt sandalwood around him. Unkept and confident, these are qualities she finds strangely alluring. Winding the window down slightly so as not to make it obvious she is reducing the strong mixture of scents, she wonders to herself, what would he look like cleaned up?

"Nice car you have," said Calum, as he glances out the window. Every vehicle on the road seems to be either white or grey in colour.

"Thanks. So, why...you to South Korea come?" Halla replied, determined to know more about her new found friend.

"To meet you," Calum said, satisfied to find something clever to break the ice.

"Oh, that's nice. We meet at last," she replied.

"My name is Calum, but most people call me Calum. That's Calum with a C," he said, using a line he had heard somewhere before.

"Halla, but most people call me, Halla, with a H," she replied, as they shake hands.

Almost immediately they feel a connection, breaking the ice between them with humour before the first set of traffic lights. There is an instant easiness in the way they relate. Two people whose paths had crossed only half an hour earlier are suddenly moving through the universe together. Now, the potential of the future is vastly different to the start of the day.

The white Honda weaves its way through traffic. Halla is a capable, impatient driver. He notices her khaki cargo shorts expose her legs from the mid-thigh downwards, showing her knees and slim white calves. He thought he had better not get caught studying that area too long.

Calum wonders where he is being taken. Some forty minutes later, across a bridge and down a winding road, they drive into a parking area beside a large reservoir. A vast stretch of water spreads out to the mountainous background as they walk around the grassy picnic area. Lotus flowers line the water's edge.

"This is called Paldang dam." said Halla. "It supply the city with water," she added.

"It's beautiful...and big," replied Calum.

Halla's arms are out-stretched beside her, absorbing the air and feeling the open space of nature. "I love it up here," she said. "Sometimes I need to go away from city, the traffic...away from people."

"I understand that. Me too," Calum said. "I like to contemplate and think about the world, my life...where I've been, where I am going." He drew a deep breath of fresh mountain air, glancing off toward the shimmering lake.

Halla threw him a smile. She must interrogate this man more to confirm her suspicions of who she thought he might be.

"I am a bit of a dreamer," he continued. "Cigarette?" he motions a packet her way, having noticed a vape on the dashboard of her car earlier.

"No thanks, but I will have vape with you."

Another sign is presented to her. First the bridge. Now he smokes. She ponders this coincidence. Is it the magic of the universe recreating art in real life?

Calum wonders how suddenly it came to be that he is almost an hour from his hotel with a foreign woman he hardly knows. He has taken another risk. She is an unknown quantity. It is unusual for a lone woman anywhere in the world to give a lift to a complete stranger. Even more uncommon for a Korean lady on her own. He found they are usually shy people, unwilling to initiate conversation, partly because they like to be perfect, he thought. If their language skills are limited, they don't want to make it obvious, by engaging with foreigners.

"Excuse. I will be back. Wait please," said Halla, making an exit to a cafe area.

"Sure," he replied, curious about her sudden departure.

Calum feels it is prudent to be wary. Like women, men have to be careful when travelling. She could be a decoy. A group of armed men might violently hustle him in to a car demanding a ransom. Will he find himself tied up in a secret shack in the Korean mountains, fed for months on a handful of rice while his captors negotiate with the Australian embassy? Men use their physical senses, women, their intuition. He decides to utilise his peripheral vision as a means of self-protection. Perhaps there is a hidden agenda. She seems to be away for a long time. However, he has promised himself to have a life of adventure and to live every day to the fullest. This is shaping up to be one of those opportunities.

Calum is starting to feel uneasy when suddenly, Halla arrives back beside him, startling him.

"I am back," said Halla.

"Ughh! Oh, there you are. I wondered where you had got to," Calum replied.

"Let's walk a little. It nice here," said Halla.

"Ok. So, boyfriend. Do you have one?" Calum asked.

Halla lowers her head and looks away. "No, no boyfriend."

"No boyfriend, that's incredible. You're beautiful."

"I not need. Coffee?"

What was that she just said, I not need a boyfriend?" Calum wondered, but it was too late to clarify. They were on their way. "Come," she said.

They move to a nearby coffee shop where they sit, she with an iced coffee and he, with his favourite, a latte. The cafe is spotless, the staff well-groomed and attentive. Calum reflects on his own attire, feeling scruffy and unkept by comparison.

"You're a brave woman," Calum prodded.

Halla moves closer, leaning across the table slightly. "What do you mean?"

"You're a brave woman for picking up a total stranger like me and taking me way up here," said Calum.

"I studied you first," she replied. "You are older and have kind face. I go by feelings and Mongee, she like you. That was enough. I feel comfortable with you."

"Me too. It feels like we have known each other a long time," Calum replied.

"Perhaps since...forever," she added as a suggestive tease. "So, what country? Where from you?" She added.

"The land down under. Australia."

"Ahh! Kangaroo. You are kangaroo who speak little English. Like me, my English, not so good," she laughed.

The sun reflects off the nearby lake painting their eyes bright. The connection is growing, yet the trust is yet to arrive. She appreciates his candid humour. He likes her energy and the way she moves, graceful, yet slightly athletic. He is amused by her constant observation of the condition of her facial makeup. Reviewing herself in a small vanity mirror she keeps accessible at all times, she pats down her foundation, unapologetically.

"Don't worry, you look beautiful," Calum said, with the intention of allowing her to feel more comfortable with herself and with him.

"You are so charming, I like that," she replied, noticing his easy, relaxed smile. He is cheeky and witty. Wit she can appreciate, but charm, she is not so sure.

Halla has concerns of self-image constantly on her mind. Calum, unaware of the social dynamics that pervade the patriarchal issues facing women in Korea, enjoys his coffee, satisfied at finally being able to find a latte.

Halla is curious about why he is in Korea. "Why?" she said.

"Why what?"

"Why come Korea you? Are you alone?"

There is a pause, which makes Halla suspicious.

"I guess it's a stop-over really, between countries," Calum answers reluctantly.

"You mean you temporary resident here? You don't know anyone, just me?"

"Just you," He passes her an appreciative grin. "Today is my second day in Korea."

"Just me and nobody else. That's amazing. That's brave," she replied.

His words echo from deep within her memory, now replaying in reality. There is increasing evidence of a deeper connection forming in her mind. How is he able to travel to foreign countries, not knowing the language? she wonders. Could he be in trouble, escaping from someone or something? However, the big question, is he the one for her, the one from an otherworldly place? She needs to satisfy her curiosity, but how long before she will get the truth?

Calum is surprised by her level of English. He uses this to divert attention away from her line of questioning. "Wow, your English is good. Where did you learn, in school?" It appeals to him to be elusive. He believes it creates intrigue.

"Yes, in school, I not practice speaking for long time. I watch movies, romance movies. Listen to English songs. I happy you understand," she added.

"You are very good."

Thank you. Gamsahamnida. That's *thank you* in Korean."

Calum attempts to repeat the word. "Cam ta meter. Cum sa neta."

"Keep practicing," she said. "You will get it."

"Cum..sata neta, Halla, with a 'H'. I like your name. Is it a common Korean name?"

"My parents spent time in Norway. They loved it so much, they wanted to immigrate. But it not possible."

"So, is Halla a Norwegian name?" Calum asked.

"Yes, it is, but also Korean. I am a...Hey! Look the sun is setting. We go?" she diverted. Calum notices her successfully change the topic. He chose to follow up on the subject later, if he has the chance.

As they approach the car, Calum moves to the left side. He has forgotten and surprised to find the steering wheel is where the passenger seat is supposed to be. "Oh, it's a left-hand-drive," he said.

Halla is amused and points to the other side. "I will drive. You are passenger. I not sit on you...yet," she added.

Halla surprised herself delivering a suggestive inuendo so soon to a stranger. It leaves Calum with a tantalising image, a small taste of what the future may hold.

"Yes, I forgot," Calum replied. "Still getting used to this new country."

"You smoke in the car?" Calum said, searching for his lighter.

"Yes, no problem. You can," Halla replied, while navigating the vehicle out of the carpark.

"You wouldn't have a light?" said Calum.

"I would not have a light. What you mean?" Halla asked.

"Oh, I mean, do you have a light?"

"But you said, I would not have a light."

"It's ok, I found one," said Calum.

"Your funny," said Halla.

"Cum sa ta meter," Calum replied.

"Gam-sa-ha-mnida," she corrected.

Why did he say I would not have a light, when he wanted one? she thought. What are the odds. Hardly anyone smokes anymore. She pictures the scene of the two of them together in a different dimension, a precious, surreal place where everything is perfect and predictable.

The late afternoon traffic is building as the sun descends, the sky turning crimson and mauve. From behind the clouds, flashes of sunlight define the sharp angular contours of Calum's face, his greying beard highlighted in the shine of the twilight rays. It is those deep blue eyes that draws Halla's attention. His stained t-shirt distracts her momentarily. Probably coffee, she guesses. He still has not told her, she thinks to herself. Is he who she thinks he might be?

"So, you no tell me. Why alone to Korea you?" Halla asked.

"It's a secret. I can tell you, but only you."

"Ok, tell me Calum, Mr Calum with a C. I waiting." Why this is so difficult for him?

"Well ok. After a 20-year marriage, I am separated. A little embarrassed actually."

Halla turns and listens intently.

"Most separations happen around the ten to fifteen-year mark," Calum continued. "We got past that, but the number twenty brought it all to an end." He shifts in his seat uncomfortably. "Got married too young."

"Traffic this time of day is...not so good," Halla replied.

"Traffic?" Calum wonders if she has heard him. The subject came to an end abruptly. It seemed to be of such intense interest to her. Suddenly, the answer lacks anything of value. This lady is a bit strange, but I like her, he thought. "Yes, it's very busy," he added.

Halla is unsatisfied with the answer. If he is, who she thinks he might be, then how can there be a previous marriage? As she ponders his response, she glances in her rear-view mirror, realising she urgently needs to increase her speed. Someone is following them.

"Oh, are we in a hurry?" Calum said, noticing the sudden acceleration, along with Halla's change in mood.

"No, Sometimes I like to drive fast," replied Halla, disguising her anxiety. "It's fun," she added.

"Sure, but can we keep at least two wheels on the road?" replied Calum, her unease becoming contagious.

The white Honda weaves its way amongst the busy afternoon traffic down the 3-lane highway towards the city. Calum revisits the idea of desiring an adventurous lifestyle, thinking it should not include becoming air-borne at 130 kilometres an hour.

"I don't believe I am having as much fun as you," he says.

An expert driver, Halla is skilled at evasive tactics. She negotiates her vehicle between small gaps in traffic at high speed, to the displeasure of other motorists.

"They are blowing their horns at us. It must mean they either know you or, a little bit annoyed," said Calum, trying to ease his own anxiety with humour.

"No, I don't know them," she replied.

A random vehicle does the unexpected. Distracted momentarily, Halla is forced to brake suddenly. With wheels locked and tyres screeching, they are out of control. Like a seasoned rally driver, Halla swerves, missing the car by inches.

"Are you feeling ok Halla? Is something wrong?" said Calum.

"It's complicated," she replied. Relieved her pursuer has given up the chase, she gives a sigh of relief. "Your hotel?"

"Yes, sure. It's a bit further along, opposite Olympic Park. I think you turn up there at the lights," said Calum. Although disappointed the day is coming to an end, he is relieved to make it back without being abducted, tortured or involved in a six-vehicle pileup, yet his encounter with her has him intrigued.

They turn down a narrow laneway, stopping outside his accommodation which has no distinguishable identifying name, an indicator of its popularity. Calum fumbles his way out of her car on to the footpath, where they maintain eye contact. Then, simultaneously they break free from each other's gaze as the driver of a vehicle behind her toots his horn impatiently.

"I really enjoyed your company," Calum said, as her car is forced to move.

"It was wonderful day," Halla said. "But please, don't come look for me," she added unconvincingly.

Calum is perplexed by her parting comment, feeling the urge to chase after her. He watches for several minutes as her car disappears down a narrow lane turning into a side street.

"Damm! Calum cursed. "I don't have her number."

He has missed an important detail, chastising himself for being so remiss. That's the basics. Get their contact info. He doesn't know where she lives or how to find her again. It's a big city. There are millions of people here. He just wants one, her. Her final elusive comment intrigues him as he turns toward his hotel, dragging his feet into the foyer area.

Halla could see him in her rear-view mirror as she drives away. "I cannot involve him in my life. Not yet," she said, regretfully. An ache forms in her heart, an overwhelming curiosity compels her to drive around the block to see him one last time. By the time she returns, Calum has gone.

As Calum catches the lift, he is greeted by one of the hotel staff.

"Hello, Mr. 7.30," Calum said, amused the accommodation manager had chosen an English name like 7.30 for himself. He wonders if it is AM or PM.

He returns a smile. "Did have good day?"

"Yes, the best ever," Calum replied.

The hotel room has only just enough space for a bed which extends under a narrow table, above which, is a small window. It is budget accommodation, far from commodious or luxurious, where the only bathroom is shared with about 10 other people who stay on the same floor. The walls, a musty yellow, cry out for a repaint. Extending across a sea of grey buildings, which he could just make out through the tiny opening, the view is a reminder he is in a huge city. He thought about the millions of people living under the omnipresent threat of their North Korean neighbour. Laying down on the hard bed, he revisits the events of the day. How did he manage to get a date with a beautiful Korean princess, and then let her escape. The sudden high-speed dash through the city for no apparent reason intrigues him. "It's complicated," he repeats her comment. Intuitively he knows something is started, but not yet finished. Again, he reprimands himself about his oversight.

"How stupid," is his final comment for the day.

Mongee greets Halla at the door, jumping and bouncing around with excitement as always. "You're so loyal. I love you," said Halla. But Mongee has her fooled, leading her to believe she is missed when the reality is, her pet feels insecure about not having anyone around for company. Dogs are pack animals. It is destabilising for them to be on their own. She scoops her up, covers her with affection and then hears her cat meowing. Songee, is also looking for attention. Sprawled out on a couch, she rolls on to her back inviting Halla to rub and stroke her soft furry underbelly. The pets have spent the day alone with each other, a rare occurrence, as Halla has not ventured far from her unit for over a year. Her animals are her family. She lives alone, close to the Han River.

In the aftermath of her encounter, the world shimmers with new-found meaning. It is this new connection brought about by chance. Has she constructed an altered reality around this casual meeting? Is it in her imagination how the fantasy of her favourite dream is being replicated? She wonders if she will ever see him again and more importantly, should she, considering her circumstances.

She throws a glance toward a photograph of an elderly couple that have a family resemblance. "It's ok, I not need relationship. I have survived so far without men," she said, in an attempt to satisfy the imaginary concerns of the people in the photograph. But is he the one for me? she ponders.

She pictures Calum's face and the muscular proportions of his arms and shoulders. Her thought process is interrupted, with the realisation Mongee has urinated on her bed.

"Mongee! she cried, not having time to find a suitable cursing word in English or Korean.

Chapter Five

The sun rose, wrapping shadows stealthy across the city. Calum woke early to search the streets for coffee, as most Australians do. He can survive without food but, caffeine is a necessity. He notices there is very little activity in Seoul in the morning, save for the occasional early-riser. Most Koreans like to start the day about 11.00am. Perhaps that is the reason for the nick-name, *'Land of the Morning Calm'*, Calum thought. The cafe he knows is closed. Thankfully, he finds one open a short distance away.

"May I have a latte?" he asks, eager to start the day. However, it's the misinterpretation of the word that forces him to settle for whatever style is presented. He knows he won't be coming back to this cafe after tasting the excessively strong and bitter brew.

As Calum sits outside the cafe, a man strolls by walking his dog. An idea strikes him, a stroke of genius, he thought. Dogs and dog parks go together. He quickly finishes whatever he can of his coffee to set off on a mission. That's where he will seek her out. He will go to every dog park in Seoul if he has to, until he finds her again. He commits himself to the cause, his obsession overriding her request not to seek her out.

He devises a strategy; follow a stranger with a dog wherever they go. They will eventually lead him to his lost princess. He follows a beagle, a labrador and a sausage dog. Much to his bemusement, it occurs to him his sight-seeing excursions of Korea includes unplanned visits to numerous dog parks. They have too many orifices, he thought to himself, noticing their owners picking up after their pets. If it's not coming out one end, it's coming out the other.

His search reveals nothing. Increasingly, she is becoming just a memory of what might have been.

It is late morning when Halla climbs out of her bed. After spending most of the night cleaning her one-bedroom unit, her fingers ache. There wasn't time to eat, with so much to do. She wonders what Calum is doing. They didn't share plans about spending another day together. Her final comment to him is regretful. Breakfast consists of a bowl of rice. She forces herself to eat, her appetite, having long since vanished.

"Is he the one for me?" the weight of the question refuses to leave Halla. Her mind lingers on the new encounter. Mongee brings her back to reality by jumping on her lap. "Mongee. Do you want to go for walk?" she said, as she pats her pet's scruffy head. This causes a high level of excitement and anticipation, her dog being fluent in the native 'Hangul' language. As though suddenly regaining her youth, Mongee runs to the door and picks up a lead in her mouth. Shaking it vigorously, she returns to Halla to show her impatience.

I wonder, what are the possibilities?" Halla thought.

Choosing a hat that conceals much of her face from the sun, as well as from those who may recognise her, she confers with her dog. "What do you think Mongee? Tell me which way I should go?" With that, they are out the door and moving down the steps. She hopes to be inconspicuous amongst other members of the dog walking community.

Calum is exhausted, his left hip killing him. Age is beginning to creep up on him after years of fighting off its relentless hunt. "What are the chances," he said out loud to himself. "Surely, it's worth a shot. If it's meant to be."

Could she have set out looking for him? Is she waiting for him on the park bench for his return?

These questions niggled at Calum. Checking Google maps, the location he seeks is about one kilometre. With a steady pace, shrugging off the pain, he sets off in the direction of the Han River. He wonders what forces are required for their paths to intersect twice, in as many days.

Chapter Six

The park bench has not moved an inch. It waits for him, a witness to his solitary musings.

Calum ponders his future. Is this the best I can expect for the rest of my life, he thought, waiting for someone to come and fill the void? He looks in the direction where he last saw Halla. Yesterday seemed a dream where the world radiated possibilities. Now, he feels trapped in his solitude. He longs for a reconnection, a bond that will anchor him to the present, sweeping away the shadows of his past. Halla has briefly illuminated his life, leaving him inquisitive and intrigued. Now, he yearns for more of her.

The vicissitudes which have recently surrounded Calum, compel him into contemplation. Watching the river, he wonders where it comes from and where it goes. For a moment he tries to picture himself being the river. Every drop of water is moving, yet the river itself remains. It is still there, being replenished. Could he, like the river, find a balance between movement and stillness? Could Halla replenish his life or will she just fill a vacuum? Can a vacuum be filled with another vacuum?

His friends have advised him that now is the time to learn to be alone. You are at the age where you should be content with your own company, they said. He found no solace in it. Like Halla's dog, Mongee, he is a pack animal, a social creature, yearning for the comforting presence of others. He cherishes the art of conversation. Calum needs people around him.

Having a variety of interests, including bird watching, he glances up to see two Oriental Honey Buzzards flying together above the river. "How fitting" Calum said to himself. They are looking for something to eat, like a couple of love birds out in search of a tasty restaurant. He might be next on the menu, he jokes to himself, looking up the river for more species. As winter approaches, the Cinereous vultures will be navigating their way here from the north, hungry and ready to feast.

Then, Calum thought he heard something familiar.

"Huh," he murmured. Is it the sound of his name being called, a whisper on the wind? Perhaps it is just his imagination, a trick of the rustling leaves of the shoreside trees. It came again, more distinct this time.

"Calum!" Halla shouts from behind him.

"Oh my God! It's you!" Calum exclaimed. "It's you, Halla, with a H." He gives her a welcoming smile.

"What are you doing here?" she said. "It is so hot in the sun."

"I am waiting for you to come, and there you are! I thought I had lost you."

"Oh. How long you here?" She said.

Calum pointed at his watch. "About 10 minutes. Perfect timing for you to arrive. I was just about to get out of the sun."

"Come into the shade. It's too hot," she scolded. Halla waves a small fan vigorously in the direction of his face to Calum's amusement. He notices she is sweating and looks adversely affected by the heat. They move to a shaded park overhung by Ginkgo trees.

"I am so happy to see you. Calum said. Are you feeling ok?" he added.

"Not really, It's my condition. I not have good .....sta...stamina in this temperature," she fumbles with the pronunciation.

Visibly upset and embarrassed, Halla retrieves a tissue from her handbag using it to remove sweat from her forehead and face. Perspiration is running down her cheeks. Looking pale and somewhat anaemic, she sways, indicating her balance is off centre. Mongee sprawls herself out on the ground, her abdomen, cooled by contact with the pavement.

"Let's go. I take Mongee home and meet you over there in that cafe soon." She points in the general direction of a coffee shop. Urgently wanting to separate from Calum and worried what he might think of her appearance, she walks away, granting herself the space to cool down and regain composure. Hurrying makes things worse as more sweat begins saturating her hair.

"Are you sure you are alright?" Calum shouts after her. Halla waves without turning. It's not the first time this has happened for her.

Calum wonders what causes her to sweat so excessively. He wants to give comfort and reassurance, but she is gone in a flash, shielding herself from embarrassment. Unable to shake the image of her face glistening with perspiration, he questions the cause. It isn't hot enough to work up that much perspiration from walking her dog, given Mongee's age. Her sweating looks as though it is as a result of having done a heavy physical work-out. He remembers his sister had similar symptoms when going through menopause. Wondering if Halla is old enough for that to happen, he estimated her to be in the mid 40's, however one can never tell with Asian women. They seem to defy time.

After crossing the road, he takes a moment to do some research on Google;

'Excessive facial sweating'.
There are several reasons why a person will have excessive sweating in the face, including infections, hyperglycaemia, tumours, medications, stress, and withdrawal from medications or drugs.

"Jeez, I forgot to get her number again," he sighed.

The cafe owner recognises him, pre-empting him to the order. "Lat tee, one shot, right?" she inquired.

"Tea please. Cum sa neta," Calum replied, making a poor attempt at pronouncing *'thank you'* in Korean.

He makes a mental note of how the owner pronounces 'latte', *Lat tee*. He chose a table, soon finding himself engaging in conversation with two elderly ladies who, with limited English skills, are not shy about attempting to converse. They are eager to speak to him, having heard him attempt Korean. "Where from? one of the ladies asks.

"Korea," he said with a smile. "Just joking. Australia."

"Oh, Australia...very far. Korea. You like?" the other lady commented, hoping for a positive reply.

"Love it. The people are so friendly. It's beautiful here in Seoul," said Calum.

''Can I take photo?" the other lady asked, holding up her mobile in Calum's direction.

"Sure," Calum replied.

While the other lady distracts him in conversation, a photographic image of Calum's characteristic grin is sent from the lady's phone with an accompanying text.

From Australia

Chapter Seven

Halla arrives back at her unit. She is flustered and upset, her emotions in disarray.

"I need to regain control of myself," she murmurs, trying to steady her trembling voice. "I hate this! I hate you!" she said.

Halla finds it difficult to handle changes in her daily schedule, feeling anxious when pressured to move urgently. Calum is waiting for her and she desperately wants to return to the cafe before he encounters someone else. "That's not going to happen is it," she promised. "He is mine...that is, if I want him." She gives herself a pretend hi-five to her reflection in the mirror. The shower is invigorating, the cold water pouring over her face and body. It makes her feel herself again as she recovers her composure. She wants to be normal, more than anything.

Halla stops her car outside the cafe. Calum excuses himself from the presence of the ladies and hops in the passenger side.

"Who are they?" Halla's tone is tinged with suspicion.

"Just some ladies I met," Calum replied.

"So, you waste no time, do you." Halla retorted, unable to conceal her disapproval. 'You should be more careful. Not everyone good."

The contrast between Calum's friendly outgoing personality and Halla's secretive, mistrustful lifestyle is starting to become apparent to both of them.

"We were just talking about trivial things, like the weather. Anyway, how are you doing?" Calum asked, feeling the need to defend himself, although he isn't sure why.

"I am good now. It's just the heat this time of year. I no like humidity," Halla replied. "I cannot feel comfortable. The air-conditioning is on. I feel better."

Calum knows she is lying, suspecting there is more to her discomfort than just humidity.

"Yes, so hot. I didn't realise Korea would have this kind of uncomfortable temperature," he continued.

"It's September. In October, it starts cooling down. Not long now. Anyway, how you?"

"How *are* you?" Calum corrected.

"How are you?" Halla repeated. "I want to speak English correct. You can help me?"

"Sure. Look at my tee-shirt." 'I teach English' is written in large bold lettering on the front of his shirt.

"I-teach-English. Really! Are you a teacher?"

"Well not really, I had this t-shirt printed in Thailand before I came to Korea. It is in the hope someone might approach me here and ask me to help them learn the language. I am not qualified, so, the best I can expect is to exchange teaching for accommodation."

"I see. What ages were you hoping to teach?"

"Zero to one," he said, waiting for her to get the joke.

"Zero to one. That's funny," she said. "Gu Gu, Ga Ga."

"That's it. You got it. The problem is, I should have printed it in Korean. Who is going to be able to read it?"

They both laugh. He is so quirky Halla thought to herself. He seems intelligent, yet there's a hint of gullibility. That means I can manage him if he gets out of hand.

"I think I might throw it away," he said.

"No, don't, I think it's cute. It shows off your..." Halla stops what she was about to say, hiding a glance toward his chest. "...your intelligence....one-year-old children could read it," she continued.

Calum gives her a half-smile accompanied by a slight shake of his head. "Gu Gu Ga Ga. That means, where should we go now, in baby language?"

"You're funny. I am thinking...I know. Olympic Park. It's not too far."

"Ok, you can be my tour guide." said Calum.

"And you can be my teacher, Mr Calum with a C," she laughed. "Gu Gu. Ga Ga."

"It's a deal, Halla with a H," he replied, feeling he is making progress in the budding relationship. Calum begins to sing, Radio Ga Ga, by Queen. Halla joins in, self-conscious at first, but then finds her voice.

They sing all the way to their destination, laughing as they go.

Calum and Halla wander through Olympic Park where numerous impressive sculptures command a presence.

"If you are an artist, Seoul is the place to be," Calum commented.

"This park is from the 1988 Seoul Olympics," Halla replied. "It was once the historic land of the Baekje era, a powerful kingdom ruling most of southwestern Korea, 1,400 years ago."

"It's beautiful," Calum replied, surprised to see an extensive eco-friendly forest in the middle of a huge city. "I imagine it's a popular place for residents to relax."

Halla turns toward him, her hand finding refuge on his

shoulder—an unspoken vow of affection. It is their first unofficial physical gesture. "You should never come here on a Sunday. You cannot hear your thoughts because of the sound of children. They are too noisy."

This is a lead-in to ask the question Calum is curious about. He dares to breach the barriers of her past.

"Tell me, Halla. Do you have children?"

"Children? Children annoy me." She replied.

Calum persists. So, I take that as, no?"

"No, I don't. I haven't had a relationship for ten years. Men annoy me. Children annoy me. Family annoy me," she added.

"Men annoy you! What about me. Do I annoy you?"

"You're different. You are older. You only annoy me a little bit. Young men just want...Look! There is Go-mingo," said Halla, noticing a cat nearby. "That means *cat* in Korean," she added.

"Go-mingo," Calum repeated.

He notices she didn't answer the question, but he feels he knows what she was about to say. Did she ever want children, or just never found the right person? He is left with the presumption she never married.

Halla walks carefully toward the cat, using it as a distraction. Relieved it has appeared, she kneels down to entice the nervous animal closer, her heart opening to the timid creature before her. It becomes obvious to Calum, she has an affinity with the feline species.

She turns to Calum. "I am a cat mother. If I see a cat in trouble, I help them."

"I love cats too. They are my favourite animal. I love them because they remind me of...."

"Of what?" said Halla.

Thinking quickly on his feet, Calum changes his usual response.

"Independence. I like that they can look after themselves." The cat rolls over, inviting Halla to pat her other side and then, suddenly runs off, regaining its fear of being close to people.

"Me too. Independence is most important. Not need anyone," said Halla. "To need no one," she whispers, her words, carrying the weight of a lifetime's philosophy.

She bumped into him playfully, pushing him slightly. "Not need man."

"Not need woman either," said Calum, gently returning the nudge.

They sat on some steps leading up to the street level.

"No relationship for ten years? Seriously. You have been alone for that long? Wow!" Calum probes deeper. "What about loneliness. How do you cope with that?"

"I have my cat and my dog. They are my family. And I have my work." Her voice is tinged with a hint of sadness. "I am a *4B* woman," she said, as she stands up to deliver her explanation.

"A what?" Calum inquired.

"4B. It means four things that start with No. The first one for me is saying no, no to giving childbirth."

"No to childbirth! Then what do the other three mean?" Calum asked.

"Next, no dating," she replied.

"So where does that leave us?"

"You and me? Friends, just friends," replied Halla.

"Ok, a friendly tour guide together with a friendly English teacher. That's us," he said.

"Yes, just friends," she said, as she returned to sit on the steps next to Calum.

"Oh, that means I can find another girlfriend and still have you as a friend?"

Halla is cornered. "No! Not allowed! You better not". She grabs his hand and squeezes.

Calum receives the first of many Korean cultural lessons. He is distracted before finding out about the meaning of the remaining two *4Bs*.

"You are not working today?" he said.

"Do you mean, Am I working today? Australians! Do you speak English in your country? Really! You are not working today. Is that a question?"

"Yes, it is. Well, are you?"

"So funny! No, not working. I have been studying one year. I have just got my qualifications in counselling."

"Well done. Congratulations."

Calum wonders how she is able to navigate life alone. She has a reasonably new car, pays for a unit on her own and presumably, hasn't worked for over a year.

"So, what career did you have before, when you were young. I mean younger?" Calum said, correcting himself.

"I was fashion designer, but I not do for long time."

"Oh, I would love to see some of your work," he replied.

"That life finish. Long time ago," Halla said, a regretful tone to her voice.

"Humm, interesting. A fashion designer."

And you? What are you? No, I should say. You are not retired?" She laughs. "That's a question."

"Well, I am sort of retired. I travel and live off the rent of my house in Australia." His advice from friends, never impart too much financial information.

"What you do before?" Halla said.

"It should be, what did you do before. Correct pronunciation."

"Oh, Thank you. What did you do before?" Halla repeated.

"I have had several lives. I was a film maker for many years," Calum replied.

"Really! Would I have seen anything you have done?"

"Probably not. Mainly commercial work and the odd documentary."

"Documentary? What about?"

"I made one on the paranormal, based on a personal experience I had with a ghost," Calum replied, unable to mask the complexity of his past.

"Wow! The paranormal. I have that happen to me a lot. I hear voices. See things...faces. Nature talks to me," Halla replied. "So, what else do you do, in your many lives?" she smiled, moving the conversation away from her.

"I was a photographer and a visual artist. Now, I am a writer."

"A photographer? Really," Another sign is presented to her, she thought. More confirmation. The bridge, smoking and now this. She cannot be contriving this in her imagination. Reality becomes increasingly blurred, every time she sees him. A photographer, for national geographic perhaps. Privately, she thanks the synchronicity of the universe, of which she feels intimately connected.

"Are you ok?" Calum asked.

"Sure, I am." But Halla is preoccupied. Calum watches her. Strange lady, he thought to himself. What is going on in her mind? So unreachable. So distant.

"Halla! come back to me. Where are you? Earth to Halla," Calum called.

Halla returns from her day dream. "I am ok. Just dreaming about something. I go off sometimes into...not sure where." She isn't ready to share the complexity of what she is experiencing, keeping it hidden in the shadows of her mind. Not yet. She needs more time to contemplate the dynamics. How strange this encounter is, she thought.

"A photographer, a film maker, and a visual artist. You are a busy man. Tell me, what do you write about?" she prodded.

"The Maya civilisation mainly," he replied. "The mathematics of their architecture. I have an interest in some alternative things."

"Oh! Mesoamerica. You write about Mesoamerica. That's interesting."

Calum is shocked she knows the word. "I am impressed. You know that word! You're educated and intelligent."

"Gamsahamnida. I read a lot." she smiled.

"I am researching another book at present," said Calum.

"Oh, what subject?"

"I am interested in studying feminine Goddesses and Deities from different cultures and ancient history," he replied.

"Oh really! The power of the feminine. Do you know about Jacheongbi? She is important goddess in our culture."

"That's one of the reasons I am here, to learn," he replied.

"She is the divine feminine. The Goddess of love and sacrifice." she said. "All women have her inside them. Perhaps you will meet her while in Korea...but will you recognise?" she added. Her statement causes Calum to ponder.

Halla is becoming vague and aloof. "Halla with a H! Here I am, over here." Calum tries to call her back from her mental preoccupation.

She looks down and away. "I am concerned I am falling for you."

"Me too," Calum replied.

"But I cannot let that happen." Halla said.

"Just go for the ride, and see where it leads. Remember, just friends." Calum is trying to convince himself as well. "I have learned not to plan anything in life anymore."

"No, I suppose not. No plans. I not need men," she added for amusement.

She laughs while Calum plays along with the mood. "Not need women. Hey, I wanted to share a song with you," he said, retrieving his phone from his pocket.

"Sure," said Halla.

Calum searches on his playlist where he finds, 'Love is in the Air' by John Paul Young. Halla has not heard the song before, humming along with the tune as she edges beside him, close enough to touch.

Once again, they are side by side, but this time a lot closer. Two souls on the same pathway, not knowing where the journey will lead. The delicate balance between their energies, invisible threads, pulling them closer. Serenaded by the melody, they know there is a special kind of magic, the lure of destiny at work. Yet, there are also circumstances and personal self-defence mechanisms, threatening to keep them apart.

"I like." she said. "Love is in the air. I like a lot."

"Calum, I have spoken to friends who have been to Australia. They said Australians are racists. Is that true?" she inquired.

Calum is suddenly on the back foot. He feels the need to protect his nationality, therefore himself. "Australia is made up of people from all over the world," he replied. "Chinese, Americans, Italians, even Koreans. Many of these people are citizens, so it's a bit difficult to say Australians are racists. You would have to include all nationalities as well," said Calum, pleased he is able to arrive at an effective deflection. He is also surprised at how quick she is able to move from the topic of love to an indirect negative accusation.

"I see," said Halla. "I understand that."

But reality is a persistent intruder, reminding Halla of her responsibilities. The passage of time prods her to speak. "I need to go home."

She is also starting to feel the effect of the humid air and with that, her facial temperature rising.

"Home already. So suddenly?" Calum lamented.

"I have a dog and cat to look after. I have responsibilities."

"Oh yes, I forgot. Ok, let's go. But please, can I have your phone number?" he said, relieved she hasn't escaped this time. It reminds him, he must get a local sim card.

"Sure, your phone please? I will put," she replied.

Calum places his phone in his pocket with a feeling of confidence. He has succeeded in establishing a permanent connection with his new-found-friend.

Halla's car comes to a stop in front of Calum's accommodation.

"How about coming back later and we will go out tonight?" Calum asked.

"Ok, that's a date," she smiled. My friend," she added.

"I am on the 5th floor. Number 102. You can come up if you like, but don't expect too much in the way of luxurious accommodation. I'm a little bit embarrassed about it."

"Ok, don't be. I know you traveller," her voice laced with understanding. "See you about 6 o' clock."

With that promise hanging in the air, they part.

In the isolation of his room, Calum finds himself lost in thoughts of her. He wonders if fate has brought them together, a reason beyond both their understanding. He had only waited for her ten minutes by the river and the synchronicity of their meeting again so quickly, astounds him. Halla stirs something deep within him, a sense of connection that defies logic. Sometimes virtually unreachable, a mystery, a puzzle he is determined to unravel. Fearing his eagerness might push her away, he knows he should approach with caution, yet her secrecy heightens his curiosity. Is her evasive nature a deliberate allure, a spellbinding technique designed to kindle his desire to know her deeper. He knew that technique well. But love, like the river he had contemplated earlier, flows in mysterious ways. He is determined to follow its course, wherever it might lead.

Halla retrieves her sheets from the dryer. "Mongee. No more of this please! I can't take it!"

She lays back on her bed, picturing what Calum might be doing at the same moment in time. "Who are you? Mr. Calum with a C," she said out loud, wondering how he made his way into her life. "Come on Mon-gee, let's go for our walk."

Mongee doesn't take any convincing. Even though she has walked the same footpath numerous times, she takes an interest in everything. Every day, the sights and sounds are new to her. There are always different people walking past she has never met.

Halla thought about Mongee as she strolls along beside her. How does she find adventure and something new to explore every day? She examines her own reclusive life and recognises the contrast. She has finished her on-line counselling qualification and yet, there is not the sense of achievement she hoped for. After meeting Calum there is a different energy about the day. He is never far from her mind ever since the first time she saw him. He has brought a quality and interest to her life that she has not known for so long. "Love is in the air." she proclaims loudly, making sure there is no one around. However, a deep-rooted anxiety surfaces. She wonders if he will be able to understand, after he finds out who she really is.

She remembers Calum telling her about his book on the Maya civilisation. She imagines him swinging through the jungle with a large boulder rolling after him, comparing him to Indiana Jones. Her imagination consumes her when suddenly, behind her, a loud rumbling sound approaches, scaring her and her dog. Several adolescents on roller skates overtake her on the concrete footpath.

"Ughuhh, I not need men!" she cried. For Halla, sometimes dream-like states merge with reality.

Why is he so ambiguous? I still don't know why he is here. I will find out tonight. He is not going to escape without me knowing everything.

Today, Mongee's alertness is more active than her master's, who is preoccupied with thoughts of Calum. A low growl and a threatening stance cause Halla to return from her musings. Up ahead, a man is walking, who she recognises. He is unaware he is seen in the crowd. Halla does a complete about-face, hurrying in the opposite direction.

"Good girl, Mongee," said Halla. "They are coming closer," she whispered.

Being in public for her is often traumatic. She longs to be carefree, enjoying the fresh air, people watching or, just visiting restaurants. A recluse for many months, the feeling of liberation, is lost to another time and place. Usually hypervigilant and observant, today she dropped her guard. A fugitive in her own city, she clings to the thought that possibly Calum may be the key to release her from bondage.

Chapter Eight

Calum and Halla are the only people in the restaurant when a large plate of raw fish arrives along with a selection of tasty spices. There is enough for four people, Calum thought. Then the beer comes, accompanied by a bottle of traditional soju, a popular fermented rice spirit.

Calum notices what she is wearing, a blue jean jacket that has a section of stiches neatly removed on one side, drawing attention to appealing horizontal lines. He admires her attire, genuinely appreciating her artistic sensibility. His eyes trace the contours concealing the roundness of her breasts. "I really like that jacket you are wearing. Is it one of your designs?"

"Yes, it is. I still make a lot of my own clothes, just for myself," she replied, her eyes sparkling with modesty and pride.

"Very artistic. Very tasteful. Not too much. Just right. I thought you were artistic when I first saw you."

"Gamsahamnida, Halla replied.

She places two small glasses on the table. "Now you in Korea, you must learn how to do things here, the right way. Next Korean girl you take out, you can impress with your cultural knowledge."

"Next girl? The next girl I take out will be you. Only you, Miss

Halla with a H. Only you," Calum replied. "Remember you are the only girl I know here in this country."

"In Korea, that is," She pauses. "We don't know how the script gets written for us."

"The script? What script?" Calum inquired.

"Please watch carefully. Place one hand on your arm on the inside of your wrist like this. It's a sign of respect. Or, you can have left hand open on your heart, like this." Halla demonstrates the process with the skill of a professional.

Calum watches carefully, appreciating the chance to get an education on local etiquette. Halla hands him a glass full of Soju. "Geon bae!" she said. "This is our way of giving a toast. Now you say. Then we drink."

Calum raises his glass to connect with hers. Geon bae!" he said.

Halla turns and covers her mouth with her hand, as she drinks all the contents.

"Why do you cover your glass with your hand when you drink?" he asked.

"You are older. It is our Korean custom," she replied, as she fills another glass. It shows respect. I turn away, cover my mouth and drink. Like this."

"Geon bae!" he said. Calum does not usually drink excessively however, Halla is soon filling up his glass again with soju. After a few more glasses, he starts feeling the effect.

"Each time we have a drink, we say, Geon bae. Be careful. Soju is strong drink."

"Gummy-sa-ha-mnida," Calum makes a poor attempt at pronouncing *thank you*, to which Halla finds amusing.

He feels certain she could out drink him. "Yes, soju is very strong," Calum slurred.

"Yes, very popular in South Korea," she replied.

"Tell me, Miss Halla with a H. Do you think someone else, outside of ourselves is writing the script for our lives?" he said, as he makes several attempts at grasping a piece of sushi. He chases it around the plate with his chop sticks like a hound after an elusive rabbit.

"Perhaps," Halla replied, leaving the question hanging in the air with a delicate promise of more to come. "Let me help you."

"No. I am good. It will not get away," said Calum, as he successfully retrieves a portion of food after a struggle. Elevating it to his mouth is another challenge. His clothes soon become coated with a variety of Korean spices.

"I am so messy."

"Yes, you are," Halla smiled.

"Are you enjoying your meal," Calum asked.

"Yes, I am hungry. I like so much," said Halla, surprised at the return of her appetite.

"Perhaps, just perhaps?...Do you think we can be the authors of our own life?" he persists with the previous topic. He likes the abstract direction of the conversation and is ready to engage further, however a waitress arrives with more food, breaking the flow of conversation. Usually friendly and sociable by nature, when Calum is inebriated, that characteristic is multiplied ten-fold.

"I like her a lot," he told the waitress, referring to Halla. "But I only love her a little bit, not a big bit." The waitress doesn't understand a word of what is being said. However, she follows the mood, responding with a smile.

Halla continues. "I no like. I no like. Not a little bit. In Korea, we always smile when we tell someone we not like them. Ha. ha." She thinks her comment is very amusing.

In Australia....if we no like, we...we...kiss them. So now is your opportunity. Say, I not like you, while kissing and smiling." Calum leans across the table in preparation.

"You crazy. More crazy than me." They both laugh as Halla feels the effects of the soju. "That so funny. Kiss me, I not like you. Ha Ha. Stop!"

"I not like you either," Calum smiled.

"I not like you. Kiss me." Ha, Ha." Halla beams a smile Calum's direction, while shaking her head.

Halla forgets her usual concern about how she looks momentarily. Suddenly, she finds herself, instinctively reaching for her vanity mirror, her desire for perfect facial presentation resurfacing. Laughter distracted her for a while but then, reality comes flooding back. Halla sees her reflection in the vanity mirror, intent on rectifying her make-up. A minute flaw needs urgent attention.

Calum is oblivious to any imperfections in her makeup. He loves watching her, amused by Halla's assortment of unusual mannerisms, like the shocked expression she gives her reflection. The feelings of being besotted is overwhelming him. But why so circumspect about the script comment? It seems like she is privy to a secret. He is becoming more mesmerised by her with the increased consumption of alcohol.

"You are so beautiful...so, so, beautiful," he said. "I cannot stop looking at you, Miss Halla with a H," he slurred. "How do I say, I love you in Korean?"

"Salanghaeyo," she replied.

"Oh, thank you, I love you too," Calum grins, as though he has just won a game of checkers.

There is that damm charm again, Halla thought. He can't stop himself. How many other girls has he swept off their feet. I bet I am not the only one he has used that line on.

"Oh! gam-sa-ha-mnida. Calum with a…. What letter was it again." she laughed, while masking her true thoughts. Stop! I don't like to laugh."

"You don't like laughing. Why?" replied Calum, amazed by the comment.

"No, I no like," as she points to lines either side of her eyes. "It make me old."

"Laughing is wonderful. Doesn't matter about making lines. Your eyes are beautiful. The irony." he continues. "Is not the facial effect of smiling and laughing more appealing to one's countenance than the residue left from concern and stress about ageing?" Not that Calum is particularly comfortable with the process. He sensed the pain he is experiencing in his hip would soon signal the end of travelling and his liberation stolen by the passage of time.

"You should learn more about Jacheongbi," Halla deflected. "She came to earth and fell in love with a man…a mortal. She sacrificed her life for love," her delivery, tinged with an element of resentment. "She sacrifice for a man!" she added.

The art of deflection is becoming common place for both of them. "C," said Calum, finishing her previous statement. "C is for Calum and for…Cigarette?" He motions to the exit.

"Yes, outside, we must go. Not here." They both make their way to the exit. Halla comes to a stop half way. "Calum, you go. I be there soon."

Feeling her facial temperature rise, Halla walks urgently toward the bathroom. Self-conscious, she avoids eye contact with the staff, yet she feels their gaze upon her. It is empty, much to her relief. A mirror reflects a horrified, sweaty face. After a check of her smile lines, the thought occurs to her that all the makeup in the world will not be enough to hide her physical reaction. The temperature increase comes in waves recovering faster if she calms down, however a public toilet is not the ideal place for deep breathing exercises. She notices a small stain on the wall tiles overlooked by the cleaner causing her further concern. Compelled to rectify it, a compulsion for cleanliness, just one of Halla's many burdens.

Calum is sitting outside the restaurant when Halla joins him. "Everything ok, Halla?"

"Yes, I am fine. Well no. Not really. Sometimes I feel I not belong here," she replied, as she sits next to him.

"In Korea?"

"No just here, on earth," her words sailing away with the wind. "On earth, where everything gets old and dis...dis...,"

"...Disintegrates." Calum finishes the word. "Try not to think too much, but I understand what you mean. Perhaps we are both lost, you and me," he said.

"Yes, you and me, lost," said Halla.

"That's why we are together." He put up his hand in a hi-five pose, to which she responds.

Calum lit a cigarette, as Halla puffs away on her vape. They are comfortable with the silence as they contemplate the circumstances of their lives. Her temperature has dropped, however Halla is feeling the effects of drinking excessively.

"Well tell me, you in Thailand before Korea, yes?"

"Only a few days ago actually," said Calum.

"How many girlfriends do you have there? One, two, maybe three... one in Korea, one in Thailand, one in every other country you go to?"

"None! You are the only one, beautiful lady. Just you. I not look that way. I not look this way. Just you."

She suspects it is the alcohol doing the talking for him. "All this flattery...lifting me up. I am flying and then, nothing." Laughing loudly, she imitates flapping her arms like wings and then, crashing to the ground.

He thinks she is hilarious, but the Soju is helping him see everything in a humorous light. "It's the truth. The total truth. I like you a lot. I love you just a little bit. No, I love you a lot, and like you a little bit."

"I no like. I no like you a lot. Kiss me. Smile." Halla laughs.

They could feel themselves falling for each other, a shared humour drawing them closer, ever so gracefully. It is becoming a semi-dream-like state when they are together, a confusing place where there is the potential of losing their individuality. Is this love? The falling feeling, they both wonder.

As they return to their table, Calum comments. "Halla, How much is one plus one?"

"Are you joking! I am a university..." Calum cuts her off.

"One plus one equals one," pointing to her and himself.

"Oh, right. Yes, one plus one equals one. I get it. Calum! No more drinking for you. You drink too fast. I think we should go," as she motioned toward the exit.

Halla insists on paying. They walk off together into the night, giggling and laughing, supporting each other as they wobble this way and that. "One plus one equals one" she smiled. "I not like."

"Yes, elementary mathematics. One plus one equals one."

"Not four?" said Halla.

"No, one, well.... maybe... another one or two."

"Maybe three," said Halla, following on with the joke.

She has her arm tucked around his as they walk off into the night. The sensation is sublime to be out with someone she feels attracted to. It's been almost fifteen years since she has had this connection, this closeness. Does he know? Is he reading her mind or, is his dream inside hers?

It feels comforting for Calum to have her there beside him, her breast rubbing against his shoulder. Is she conscious she is doing that? He wonders.

They stop beside a flight of steps which leads down to a lower basement level. A dimly lit karaoke bar attracts Halla's attention, a place where they would be less conspicuous, she hopes.

"And I am that other entity," whispers Halla, just loud enough to be semi audible.

What did you say?"

"Coming?" Halla said, as she tugs in the direction of the descending stairs.

Calum is reluctant, unsure where it leads. "What happens down there?" he said.

"Singing. Dancing, Come on. Let's go!" she said.

Calum holds back, assessing his capacity to make a clear judgment, being more than a little bit drunk. A strange foreign woman is inviting him down a dark flight of steps late at night to who-knows-where. What's the worst that can happen, lose a few organs perhaps.

"Arrmm," Calum murmurs.

"Are you alright, Calum? You look a little concerned. I love you. It's ok, you safe with me."

"Sure, let's go. I have my guide with me. We can fight the dragon together. Donate a few organs. I am good with that," he relented.

They make their way down the steps with Calum hanging on to the handrail with one hand and Halla, the other. Halla thinks his nervousness is amusing. Calum notices she slipped that comment in, *I love you*. Is it a bit early to say that? he thought. Doesn't a relationship have to evolve more before one member starts making such intense statements. They had only known each other two days. "Doesn't matter" he reassures himself.

"What?" said Halla. She continues. "It's ok, I will make sure you get out alive. I am your guide remember and you, my teacher." Halla touches him on the nose with her pointing finger.

They find their way to a private room with soft couches, a karaoke tv screen along with enough beer and soju to last a week.

"Geonbae!" Halla said, as they raise glasses.

"I am having so much fun, Calum. Thank you. It's because of you."

"Me too. It's because of you," he reciprocates.

"No, really. I don't go out," said Halla. "All year I study. Stay home with my cat and dog. Geonbae! Mr Calum with a C." It's because of you."

"Gum bear! Miss Halla with a .... I forget"

They laugh together.

She watches him sitting back relaxed, feeling herself drawn to his self-confidence. It is his inner courage and strength that attracts her. He lives a life without fear, which to her, would be unachievable on her own. He can go anywhere, talk to anyone, be himself without concern for favour or scorn from others. A free spirit. With him beside her, she may be able to break free of the prison walls, fear of the unknown, fear of people and even fear itself. With him, she can see her life being lived how it should be lived. She could feel it, almost touch it. It is so real, so close.

"Ok, let's dance, my teacher. I know. Unchained Melody." she said, as she sorts through a selection of songs. "You are my type," said Halla with an alluring smile. In her mind, she replays the words memorised perfectly from her altered reality; I was acting like another woman, yet I was more myself than ever before.

As Calum watches her sway to the music and singing, it appears to him, she is finding a release from a captivity that perhaps, she has imposed on herself. He glimpses a special moment of her complete free expression. It is then he sees the full vividness of her internal beauty shine. She makes him feel special, a feeling he too has not experienced for a long time. The romance left his marriage long ago. Although the love is still there, it has transformed. Their relationship evolved into a matter of practicality with the responsibility of rearing children and paying bills. The beautiful feelings of longing for each other and the need to be near, left years earlier. Perhaps, they have said all that is needed to say to each other over their time together. As painful as it is to separate, there was no recourse, but to end it. It had gone too far to rekindle those precious feelings that initially brought them together.

Now, there is this new emotion beginning to overcome him. Halla looks so beautiful, so perfect. The music, the alcohol and the lyrics magnify his emotions as the shared feelings flow effortlessly between them. They are building upon the connection of love together, the beautiful feeling of union. Nothing else matters. Time has stopped, in a room at the bottom of a flight of descending stairs, sharing a special moment together, neither of them will forget. Their thought processes are synchronised in perfect harmony with the energy and the eternity of the moment.

"That was beautiful." Halla said, as tears form in her eyes.

"What's wrong?" said Calum. "Don't cry."

"Just feeling very emotional. I miss my mother."

"Your mother?" said Calum.

"Yes, she gone for eighteen years. I miss every day. I think about all the time."

"I'm sorry." Calum reached out and holds her hand. "That must be hard. Me too. My mother is gone as well. I understand."

"It's just so hard, so long. Eighteen years. I not forget her every day. But now I feel happy, because of you."

"Perhaps, it's time. Time to let go." he suggested.

"Yes, I know I have to, but I don't want. She my earth mother," Halla lamented.

"Earth mother?"

"Yes. My earth mother," she repeated.

Calum reaches out and holds her hand again. "Our mother is such a powerful influence on our lives. I feel for you Halla. We cared for our mother, my two sisters and I. For five years she was able to live independently in her own home. We decided to help her, because she cared for us when we were small. What goes around, comes around."

"What's that mean? What goes around, comes around?"

"I suppose you would call it karma. We all take our turns at being dependent and also independent and we all have responsibility. You have a responsibility to your cat and dog," he reminded her.

Her eyes filled with gratitude. "Yes, I have." That word 'responsibility' strikes a chord with her. "I have a responsibility to them. she repeated."

At that moment, Calum doesn't realize that it will be the first and last time he will see her cry. He had recently observed the unique bond between mothers and daughters, and it resonated with him. He knows it is a different kind of love, a silent and profound connection unlike that between a man and a woman or a father and a son. Finally, he thought, she is sharing a part of her authentic self.

"And you still have your father? Is he still with you?"

"Yes. Let's dance. But first, another?" she said, enticing him with a glass of soju. They drink the contents, then she helps him up from his seat. "Listen Calum! It is playing. Our song. Love is in the Air."

"This is our song," said Calum, while struggling to remain vertical.

"Yes, I will never forget. I will never forget you." She kissed his hand. In turn, he kissed hers.

"Hey, I am booked into a hotel in Busan for three nights, starting tomorrow."

"Tomorrow! You go, already?" said Halla, feeling the weight of his absence, even before he has left.

"It will be only for a few days. I booked it before coming to Korea. I am coming back to Seoul."

"Oh, ok. You will love it there," Halla gave him a half smile trying to hide her disappointment. The thought raced through her mind that she has just found him, and now, he is going.

"Yes, I catch the train tomorrow, but I will be back to Seoul. Hey, why not come with me? I will pay," Calum pleaded.

"I cannot leave my dog and cat," she relented.

"What about leaving them with friends or, with your father?"

"They get upset when I not there. I am responsible for them. They helped me through difficult time. You go. Have fun. Enjoy Korea," she said, as she raised a toast. "You might meet new girlfriends. Not come back. There might be new script to follow."

"Halla, I am not looking for a girlfriend. Really, I am not looking. What are you talking about, script?"

Halla changed the subject. "I not love you. I not like you. Kiss me. I not like you. I love you a little bit," she laughed, as she spilled a bottle of soju over the table.

Calum stands up, about to make a presentation to an invisible audience.

"Thank you for coming everyone. We are here welcoming Halla back to the world. It's been a long time, but she has arrived. Take a bow Halla. You are back. The world has been waiting. Now you have returned. Everybody! Halla is in the house! Give her a clap!"

Calum is clapping and Halla is playing along by bowing, laughing and waving. "Stop! You crazy. You too crazy for me. More crazy than me." She gave him a 'hand to the ear and mouth' gesture. "Call me from Busan." I wrote my email, just in case. Now you have no excuse."

"Halla, I won't forget...I will never forget you... I don't like you," he smiled.

"Yes, Love is in the air. I don't like you either." said Halla playfully. "I don't like you ...not even a little bit...maybe...I don't like you...A little, but I like you a lot."

Although they are close together in the dimly lit room, it is too soon to kiss. They both know it isn't the right time, not yet.

The night wears on, a dance of mispronounced words and emotions. With a promise to contact each other, they part ways, their hearts intertwined in a swirl of different emotions, leaving them both with a memory, a shared magical moment of their time together.

However, Halla is yet to learn of Calum's fear-the fear of being alone, while he, soon to discover the secret duality of a parallel universe she is building in her mind.

Chapter Nine

"You have girlfriend. She give this for you." Mr 7.30 gives Calum a white hessian shoulder bag with a cheeky smile and a goodbye wave. Surprised by the sudden acquisition, Calum thanks him and begins his walk to the subway.

Mr 7.30 then sends a text.

She was here. He is going Busan by train.

Navigating the intricate maze of the subway network in Seoul will be a test, he thought. Very few people can speak English and those in the ticket office hardly knew a word. Follow the red line all the way to Seokchon, then transfer to the grey line to Dongjak. Finally, the blue line goes to Seoul Station. From there, its smooth sailing all the way to Busan. This is going to be difficult, he thought, with all the foreign-name places. Thankfully each train station has English sub text.

Travelling alone is a challenge he set for himself. He needs to know he is still able to navigate his way around the airports and train stations of foreign countries, a personal test to maintain self-confidence. Amidst the foreign signs and hurried footsteps, he wants to prove he is still capable. If he can navigate this complex landscape, he can also navigate life and survive.

He is bemused to learn he has aged a year just by arriving in Korea, as they count from the moment of birth as one. Staring at the ceiling in a hospital bed is not an option when he gets old. He promises himself, the only ceiling he wants to see at the exit is the vault of the heavens, the sky, the clouds, and the horizon.

The train to Busan in Southern Korea rockets along at three hundred and five kilometres an hour. Beautiful scenery flies by at phenomenal speed. Now he has time to sit back and enjoy the ride. In the blur of passing landscapes, he ponders the intensity of his feelings, not anticipating falling for Halla so swiftly, so deeply. He compares his experience to the rush of the hi-speed train carrying him away.

Alone again, he whispers to himself. "What just happened?" She was not on his travel itinerary, an emotional attachment that has taken him totally by surprise, like a tidal wave washing over him. Suddenly, he feels fractured, more incomplete than before he met her. It's wrong not to have Halla with him, her absence, palpable.

It challenges him to know she was a fashion designer in an earlier life. Calum usually finds it difficult staying clean, a total mess magnet, while she is always perfectly presented. He has 3 t-shirts, one pair of shorts and a pair of jeans. He minimises luggage in order to move through airports effortlessly. Everything he carries can be stored in an overhead locker.

Despite his longing for her, he also feels an invigorating release. He is moving again. The freedom of travelling alone always opens new doors, new experiences that the non-adventurous will rarely know the glory of unseen horizons.

Thoughts of her prompts him to search the contents of the bag Halla prepared. In it are an assortment of useful travel items, tooth brush, energy bars, face washers and a back scratcher as well as an assortment of other personal items. How kind and thoughtful of her, he thought. It is more than just a hessian bag. It is a gift from someone who has captured his emotions in a whirlwind. It's contents are far from ordinary. They hold the imprint of a soul he connects with in an extraordinary way. The items have *her* on them.

He also discovers something unusual. Halla had put a satchel of feminine products in, presumably by mistake, a lotion to alleviate itching and unpleasant odours for women. What is he to do with this medicinal product, he wonders. The bag, given out of kindness, contains not only travel items, but also this evidence, the means to undertake a challenging assessment of character sometime in the not-too-distant future.

Calum is preoccupied, therefore vulnerable. Had he been concentrating on his peripheral vision, he would have known he is being watched by a clandestine figure at the rear of the carriage. But the last thing he is thinking about is, that someone would be following him. The man knows him from Calum's first meeting with Halla by the river and a photograph sent to him by the lady in the cafe. He suspects the bag Calum is in possession of contains vital secret information, perhaps travel documents and passports, a means for Halla to escape the country with him. Convinced he should follow, the man mistakenly believes that wherever Calum is, she will not be far away.

Chapter Ten

Halla's world has slowed. She didn't expect Calum to enter her life and disappear again, so suddenly. Again, she is alone with her pets. Her repetitive lifestyle comes flooding back and with that, dissatisfaction. Ensnared by the mundane routines of everyday life, his disappearance gnaws at her like razors. She is now uncomfortable with her environment having experienced the excitement of having Calum in her life. The silent walls surrounding her heighten her awareness of the separation. Ironically, it is a necessary isolation, for in her quest for personal freedom, she is compelled to build a prison for herself. There are those who would force their will on her if she were to be found. She can sense them drawing closer.

Calum does not yet have a mobile sim card, so she could not call him. The only means of communication is by email. "I will make him love me," Halla whispers.

Halla: I hope you have good time in Busan.
I met Mr. 7.30 at your hotel. Did you get the bag I left for you?

What she also really wants to say is: Make sure you don't meet a new girlfriend. She worries about that threat constantly, knowing

Calum has the looks that are attractive to Korean women. That, and the fact he is obviously a foreigner, adds another level of appeal. Not knowing if he has the travel-bag she prepared for him is bothering her. Is he lost? She knows the subway system is very complicated, especially for someone who cannot speak or read Korean.

Numerous things are running through her mind simultaneously. "I still don't know why he is here in this country." Is he just a drifter wandering from place to place without ties or connections? If so, he is potentially dangerous and destabilising for her. She has successfully designed her life to be free of the entanglements of relationships for many years, but now he has brought uncertainty. Strangely, excitement and intrigue transcends any reservations of this encounter. For her, their tryst is the birth of a magical story unfolding, the promise of a bright new adventure. It is more than a chance meeting, it's the beginning of a mysterious narrative. An enchanting subplot stalks her, awakening her senses, drawing her into the intricate web of the universe.

Her unit is in an unacceptable condition for her to feel comfortable because of her fastidious standards, despite tidying it from top to bottom only a few days earlier. She needs to do more work, before she can relax. In a cupboard, hangs a variety of fashion accessories and clothing styles, suitable for both men and women. On the upper shelf, lies a selection of men's hats, fake beards and wigs, akin to what a fugitive might have concealed. But now, there is another on-going problem. Mongee has done her business on Halla's bed again. It is a form of protest. She is making a comment, unhappy Halla spent the night out on the town. "Stop doing this Mongee!"

Chapter Eleven

Calum steps out of the train station in search of his shared accommodation at Busan, a city on the south east coast, the first international port in Korea and the closest point to Japan. His maps app refuses to provide assistance until eventually, help arrives from a local passer-by. "It's ok, I not a scammer, I help you," said the stranger.

This not-so-reassuring comment makes Calum feel uncomfortable. "That's nice. I can relax now you have said that," Calum said.

Even with the dubious reassurance that came with this new found acquaintance, he proves a valuable asset. With his help, Calum is able to find his well-hidden abode.

His accommodation is one small room shared by five other people less than half his age. As he climbs on to the upper bunk, he convinces himself he will deal with anything that comes his way. He has learned to sleep anywhere while travelling, overnight in a Chinese graveyard in Malaysia, a grass hut in Guatemala, and on the side of the road in Australia. A dry bed with air conditioning is more of a luxury than a problem.

Halla is never far from his mind, a comfort that transcends the cramped confines of his lodgings. How is this relationship going to succeed anyway, he thought, as obstacles confront him. She would not endure this kind of discomfort, he mused. He is a leaf in the wind. She, a lone wolf, who finds comfort in the stability of an organised life. Their relationship is a conundrum, a puzzle yet to be solved. She, with her structured life, and he, with his nomadic spirit.

Now separated, they both have the feeling of being incomplete. It is a strange uncomfortable disturbance to their life they both share.

> *Calum*: I found my hotel. Thank you for the gifts. Humm, Am I having a good time? The truth is, you are on my mind all the time. There is a certain emptiness. Sorry to say that and embarrass you. I would love to have you next to me...to complete my circle.

Busan has a different energy to Seoul, more like a tourist attraction in Thailand, than what he saw elsewhere in Korea. Amidst the Chinese and Russian merchants lining the streets, Calum finds a reflection of his own internal turmoil, far removed from the cleanliness of Seoul. Still, it is new, a different place to navigate and explore.

Halla hangs by her computer, breathless, waiting for a message, anything that will soften the blow of his absence. Love, she knows, is never a smooth voyage; it can be a tempest, a whirlwind that sweeps away the familiar and ushers in the unknown. Yet, in that moment, she chooses to brave the storm, for within its chaos, she is intuitively aware what her soul needs, to feel the breath of life again. Her words carry a hidden plea, a subtle message of needing him in her life.

> *Halla*: Did you have a good time today?
> I miss you, Calum!
> You must be so tired.
> I was worried if you found the Hotel well.
> I called the Hotel because, there was no way to contact you.

They refused because it was personal information.
I'm glad you arrived safely.
You must be tired, so take a rest.

Strolling along the public beaches which attract thousands of tourists to Busan from across Korea and abroad each summer, Calum notices the stark differences that unfolds before him. The local swimmers, adorned in one-piece suits, wide brimmed hats and buoyed by bright yellow inner tubes, present a feeling of modesty and tradition. The scene is in stark contrast to the sun-drenched beaches of his Australian homeland where some swimming outfits are almost invisible. He reflects on the contrast between the scene before him with the carefree familiarity of his up-bringing.

As he observes the locals, Calum's mind drifts to the romance that is weaving itself around him and Halla. A realization confronts him. It echoes of a cultural landscape that seems, in his eyes, sexually repressive, a juxtaposition to the free open-air spirit of his native land. This cultural dissonance, as he perceives it, becomes a prism through which he views the intricacies of his connection with Halla. Are the subtle nuances of reserved modesty he observes, a prelude to the trials and tribulations that might shape the future of their fledgling romance.

Emails are an ineffective form of communication, so Calum decides it is time to get a local sim card. With the help of the hotel owner, he is able to finally make connection with Halla using an online communication platform.

Calum: I found you.
Halla: I miss you
Calum: I don't like you. I love you a little bit.
Halla: Me too.

Calum and Halla are forming a private bond through an understanding of their quirky style of communication. They understand each other's way, to someone outside of their relationship, could be misinterpreted. This is a significant step forward in Calum's mind. For Halla, she recognises their humour is uniquely their own, giving her a genuine feeling of a close connection. Her personal insecurities resurface occasionally, making her prone to thinking the worst.

Halla: Are you planning on having lunch with a pretty Busan lady?

Calum recognises that her message demands a certain type of response.

Calum: There is only one beautiful lady in Korea. That's you.
Calum: Can we face time?

Halla knew that question would come up eventually. Believing she has lost her beauty with the onset of middle age, his request automatically prompts her to retrieve a vanity mirror from her handbag. She is looking for imperfections, not what is right, but what is wrong.

Halla: No, I no like. Facetime, no.
Calum: Ok, I understand. I think you look beautiful. To me, you are a work of art.
Calum: I am going to walk up a mountain to Gamcheon Culture Village to look at the view.

Her reluctance about sharing facetime suggests she has a deep-rooted problem, he thought, that of being self-conscious and insecure about her looks.

After a short train ride from the city, then a steep walk uphill to the Gamcheon Culture Village, it is there where he can see an avalanche of coloured buildings flow down the hillside. He laments Halla is not there beside him to share the view.

Halla took Mongee for a walk finding herself near the river once again. The distant Olympic bridge inspires thoughts of Calum. This is where things changed so abruptly for her. She considers the swiftness of how her life has transformed. It is unsettling, yet in the uncertainty, there is a new hope for the future.

Halla: Are you having girlfriend again?

Yes, she is jealous, Calum smiled to himself as he descends the mountain. That's nice. It means she cares. Perhaps this next comment will test her ability to see the funny side.

Calum: Sorry, do I know you?
Halla: You are the one I found near the river, Right?
Calum: Yes. Can I bring a girl I found here back to meet you?

There is a long pause.

Calum: I was joking. I love you. I don't like you.
Halla: Get some rest. You have done a lot of walking today.

The airconditioned room is a welcome reprieve from the sweltering humidity. As Calum thinks about his circumstance, he considers changing his travel plans. The separation is weighing on his ability to enjoy the Busan attractions. What is the point of being here, if his mind is constantly on his new friend so far away, he thought.

Calum: I am coming back to Seoul early. I miss you too much. I feel incomplete without you.
Halla: I have missed you too. Too much! I will meet you at the train station.
Calum: Wonderful! The train gets in at 2.13pm.

The bullet train seemed to move a lot slower on the return journey. As Calum steps off the train on to the platform, he notices a large clock displaying the time, 2.13pm exactly. The precise arrival timing amazes him.

Calum: I am at central station. See you soon at Jamsil train station.
I will text you when I arrive. Probably, in about an hour.

As it is with most new romances, the element of separation means a longing, an emptiness. The absence of each other becomes an absence of self, a solitary journey through a world, accompanied only by their own shadow. In order to fill the emptiness, they know they need to be beside each other.

Chapter Twelve

"Hey, it's you and me again, together once more, Miss Halla with a H," said Calum, settling into the passenger seat of her car.

"My kangaroo, I have missed you. My teacher is back," said Halla, as she reaches across, clutching his hand.

The need that has haunted them dissolved. In that moment, they both realize the essence of love lies not in the absence, the longing, but in the fulfillment found in the presence of the one who completes the heart's most intricate design. Two incomplete circles are whole once more.

"I wasn't sure if I would see you again," said Halla.

"I was lost without you. That's why I came back. You realise we are getting ourselves into trouble."

"Trouble? Yes, I know" It's difficult for me. I have not had relationship for fifteen years," she confided.

This comment triggers Calum's memory. He is sure she said ten years the last time, now its suddenly fifteen years. Now, he isn't certain at all what she said. Not wanting to destroy the joy of their reunion, he remains quiet about the ambiguity, saving clarification for later.

Where to? Your accommodation?" said Halla.

"Yes please, but it's a different one to the last one. A bit bigger, I hope."

"Have you seen?"

"No, not in person. I booked on the internet. I will just deal with whatever comes. It's near the Lotte World Mall, so it should be more central."

"Mr. 7.30 will be disappointed not seeing you again," said Halla.

"He will. I liked him. What a funny name. I will never forget."

In the side pocket of the passenger door, Calum finds a book that he presumes Halla is reading. "A Planet of Viruses. Are you reading this book?" he said.

"I like to read and improve my English," replied Halla.

Calum read aloud part of the back cover. "*Scientists are discovering viruses everywhere they look: in the soil, in the ocean, even in deep caves miles underground.*"

Are you interested in this topic?" he asked.

"Yes, I like to expand my knowledge on many subjects," she replied.

"It's a very scientific subject. You never cease to amaze me."

"Thank you. Gamsahabnida," said Halla.

"Cumsa..ta...neta," said Calum.

Calum thought that the book would not lead to peace of mind, more likely a neurosis, especially in light of Covid 19 causing havoc on the world.

As they approach Calum's new accommodation, Halla surveys the area before finding a carpark hidden in a nearby alley. Her clandestine lifestyle, a constant preoccupation for her, with Calum, oblivious to her motives and thought processes.

Calum's lodgings are just two flights up from street level. He doesn't know what to expect, but isn't overly concerned. For Halla, it is a different matter when they enter the room.

"I surprised you not look first," she said, as they remove their shoes before entry.

"I am sure it will be ok. I am on a budget," Calum replied.

There is only just enough area for both of them. A single bed runs the full length of the room. It has a private shower, marginally bigger than his last accommodation. Outside in the hallway is a communal kitchen. Halla heads for the mirror to check her makeup.

"What do you think?" asked Calum, pleased with his selection.

Halla is unable to find any descriptive words in English, so she chooses not to answer. She wants to start cleaning the room straight away, noticing imperfection everywhere she looks, which annoys her. Calum doesn't have a problem with the level of cleanliness.

"I am going to have a shower when you are finished in there," Calum said. "I am feeling hot and uncomfortable."

"Ok, I finish soon. I wait outside for you," replied Halla. He definitely needs a shower, she thought.

"No peeking," said Calum, as Halla steps out the door into the hallway. She pretends to close the door and then opens it again slightly, to catch Calum by surprise.

"You're funny," said Calum, as they both share a smile.

He looks as good as he does in her imagination, the blue eyes, the wide shoulders. She would have loved to stay in the room, but not yet. It's too soon after his return and she doesn't want to appear like she is hypnotised.

The cold water runs across Calum's face as thoughts of Halla linger on his mind. What was it she said? Ten or fifteen years? He is surprised she accompanied him to his room. Perhaps there is something else on her mind? With a towel wrapped around him, he steps out of the shower and searches through his backpack for something clean. Halla joins him, sorting out soiled clothes from the not so soiled.

"I take home. I wash for you," she said, as she puts several items in a plastic bag.

"You don't need to, Halla, I can find a laundromat," Calum protests. Halla does not take no for an answer. She continues putting all the rest of the clothes in her plastic bag.

"Halla! what are you doing? I will need something to wear. I only have a towel."

"Oh, why?" Halla laughs.

"Your funny, I like your humour."

She is making a seductive suggestion again, Calum thought. Halla however, didn't build too much into her comment. It is more to break the ice of his sudden and unexpected re-entry into her life.

"Hungry?" said Halla.

"You should say, Are you hungry?" Calum corrected.

"Thank you, teacher. Are you hungry?"

"Not really. You?"

"I am good. Let's go for a walk around the lake."

"Ok, but I need to get dressed."

"You probably should," Halla smiled.

"Turn around please," Calum motions. Halla turns around 360 degrees, laughing. "Ok, I wait for you downstairs," said Halla, as she heads for the door.

"I don't like you," smiled Calum.

She just did it again, Calum thinks to himself. The playful covert suggestions.

With her arm tucked inside his, they set off around the perimeter of Seokchon Lake Park, a leisurely 45-minute walk. For Halla, exercise brings about a rise in her facial temperature. She consciously measures the pace, unbeknown to Calum.

"You are my type," said Halla, as she squeezes Calum's arm close to her breast.

"Your type?" said Calum.

"You are an onion. So many undiscovered layers. I like people with depth," she continued. "Yes, you are my type."

Calum stops and pulls her close. He whispers in her ear. "Can I keep you?"

Halla needs a moment to interpret the expression, never having heard it before. "Yes, I want," she said, looking away. "Can I keep you. I don't like. That is funny, so funny."

As they continue, Calum slips his hand in the back pocket of her jeans and pulls her closer. "Oh, that is uncomfortable for me walking," Halla said, as she pulls his hand out and holds it with hers.

"Oh, sorry. Stay with me," said Calum.

Halla squeezes his hand tightly. "Ok, yes, I want," she replied.

Ahead of them, a small crowd had gathered around an elderly lady sitting in the middle of the pathway. Her nose is bleeding and in a degree of distress, possibly from over physical exertion. Halla reacts with concern as does several other bystanders. Calum notices the empathetic looks on the faces of those who stop to offer help.

An ambulance had not yet been called, so he takes the opportunity to phone a paramedic he knows in Australia. Unfortunately, there is no answer. It would have been a perfect opportunity to impress Halla, making him look like the hero to the rescue, a knight in shining armour arriving in the nick of time. However, his mission failed. There is no glory in just being an observer on the scene with nothing to offer. He dialled the number again, hoping to redeem the moment, but still no answer.

The lady is helped to a nearby seat by Halla along with some other onlookers where they assist her to telephone relatives. The incident, where Calum could have gloriously participated in saving the day, ended up being a missed opportunity for him.

"We should leave now. She has contacted her family. There are too many people here," said Halla, as she grabs his hand.

"Yes. The crowd would be upsetting her more," replied Calum.

"I hope she will be alright," said Halla, a hint of concern in her voice.

"She should be, probably a bit too much exercise, my guess is." replied Calum.

The unfortunate circumstances the lady experienced, is a catalyst for Calum to unravel the layers of his own identity. He examines his perceived non-conformity with that of the powerful influential shadow of social tradition, a narrative, centuries old. A stirring within prompts him to scrutinize his life, where a conflict surfaces; his place within the stereotypical roles of men and women.

Traditionally, the man is the hero to the rescue, the provider, while women, the tender caretakers of home and offspring. Beneath the surface, a truth lay begging to be discovered—a truth that challenges not only his own convictions about himself but also, the societal norms that seek to define him. He finds himself entangled in the unspoken rules that delineate the boundaries.

"Amazing," Halla commented, as they sit down on some steps a short distance away.

What's amazing?"

"Drama." Halla's voice trailed off, but she chose not to elaborate.

The circumstances around the elderly lady, also provided an opportunity for Halla to do some introspection. The event allowed Halla to demonstrate to Calum her capacity to show empathy and support for someone less fortunate. Yet, for her, there is something missing. True sentiment is an alien emotion. She shows her feelings largely by imitating the reaction of others, mimicking expressions, but not entirely able to experience the emotion within. As a result, she has become a confident actress. However today, there is a slight difference. She genuinely felt an element of concern that is unfamiliar to her. Her psychologist had told her one of the symptoms of her mental condition is difficulty feeling empathy. Her diagnosis of mild autism weighs heavily. This is a concern for her, but more so now. If Calum is to become aware she has a mental health problem, perhaps he will be reluctant to pursue their relationship. She protests secretly to herself. Nothing wrong. Nothing wrong. They are wrong!

Calum notices Halla is wearing jeans with tears and holes, a fashion statement in Korea at the time. He finds one hole and places his fingers on her upper leg, tickling her soft, smooth skin underneath. "Halla! you have tears in your jeans. How did that happen?" he said smiling.

"Oh, these are my grandmothers, handed down in the family for many years. We are poor," she replied, playfully rubbing her eyes, imitating a crying expression.

"My Halla, I'll buy you new ones. I cannot have you walking around in public with holes in your jeans."

Halla straightens her legs out in front of her. "I put more in them. The balance wrong. I couldn't wear until I fix," Halla said, as she points to a tear. "This one and these two, I put to make right."

"Perfect balance. You made the right decision."

Calum considers now is a convenient time to pursue the topic of her income. "So, you have stopped doing fashion designing for a long while. What else have you done?"

"Me? I was a dog groomer," She retrieves her phone to share before and after pictures.

"Wow! Absolutely amazing. Such precision," said Calum.

"And these." Proud of her achievement, Halla shuffles through the images to reveal more photos of pets. "I paint," she added.

"You painted these? Wow, they are a perfect likeness of the photograph. Unbelievable!" Calum is amazed at the level of perfection. Her work is an identical replica of the adjacent image.

"It takes me long time to make perfect," said Halla.

"My Halla, the artist. What a mystery lady. You are so talented."

Halla had painted the side profile of a cat with a pink butterfly landing on its nose. "I love this one so much," said Calum.

"Gamsahabnida," replied Halla. "I will send you."

"How do I say, mystery lady, in Korean, asked Calum.

"Sinbihan yeoin," she replied.

"My sinbihan yeoin. My mystery lady. I am proud of you. Can I keep you?"

"I want." said Halla, as she cuddles closer to Calum.

"Artists have something to share with the world. Sometimes it is difficult for us to find where we fit in. Most artists need to see phycologists more than any other profession," commented Calum.

"Finding a place to fit in has been difficult for me," she shares a burden close to her heart. "Sometimes I don't know what is real from the dream. I have something to share. I am sure. Something big."

"Tell me, Halla," said Calum.

"I am her. She is me."

"I am her. She is me? How cryptic you are, my artist," said Calum, struggling with the subtle meaning and the depth of her words. "What does that mean?"

"What it says," she replied, refusing to expand upon her internal thought processes.

Calum came to Korea with his luggage however, they both travel through the world with their secret baggage. Halla harbours a professionally diagnosed condition. Provided there is little stress or any significant change in her routine, she has learned to function relatively normally. However, she wonders if she can hold it together for much longer? Already, she has moved out of her comfort zone having previously been unable to maintain a close relationship for an extended period.

Calum is in a confused state of determining if he is the pack-animal personality he admires or, really, a lone wolf completely independent of the need to be with anyone. Sometimes he seeks isolation to regain his energy. Other times, a need to have someone in his life constantly is a nagging perpetual need. These contrasting paradigms tear at his equilibrium as he engages with the world.

"Tell me about your trip to Busan. What did you see? Who did you meet?" Halla prodded.

"I hardly met anyone because I could only think of one person."

"Who?"

Calum pokes her gently in the ribs suggesting there is no need for an answer. "I saw lots of beautiful scenery out the window of the train," he replied. "Mountains, rivers, landscape that looked almost untouched. That surprises me, because you have such a long history with so many people."

"Yes, Korea is beautiful. We have everything, even active volcanoes," said Halla proudly.

"Really?" he replied.

"Yes, on the border between China and North Korea. It's called Mount Baekdu. But it hasn't erupted for a thousand years. Some say it might soon," she added. "We believe it our ancestral homeland."

"That might get rid of some people in North Korea you are not fond of. Hey! I have something for you," Calum said, as he retrieves a small package from his pocket.

"For me?" said Halla. She unwraps a small pendent and chain, a blue flower compressed in resin.

"I got it in Busan. I chose blue because it would go nicely with your jacket. Do you like it?"

"I love. The colour. It's perfect. Blue flowers."

"I will help you put it on," he said, pulling back her hair gently.

"When I wear, I will think of you."

To Halla, it is perfect. The colour, the composition, everything about the moment makes her feel connected. The pendent, a catalyst allowing her to re-enter her secret world where synchronicity finds its way to the heart of her soul. An unknown force that is a mystery to her, pulls her toward him. A riddle unfolds around her life, the uncanny parallel universe, building in intensity since the first day they met.

"Halla! Where are you? Mysterious lady," Calum said. But Halla is unable to talk. Her reply is only a gesture, a hand movement, as she taps her fingers to her forehead and points to the sky.

"Ok, I will wait for you to come back to earth," said Calum.

Across the lake in the sky, hues of violet caress crimson clouds, shifting and changing. Street lights flicker sporadically as the sun lowers. Darkness falls gently, like a silken twilight sheet across the Korean cityscape. People parade beside the water's edge murmuring of the past, sharing visions of the future. The shimmering luminosity of reflections, signal ambient messages of love and beauty upon the tranquil scene.

"Come, let's lay here on the grass and look up at the stars," said Calum.

Unaccustomed to laying directly in contact with the earth, Halla is hesitant. She thinks there are crawly things, ants, beetles and all kinds of undesirable beings in the grass.

"Come on Halla. This is what lovers do. They talk about the universe and our place in it," Calum said with a smile, recognising her reluctance. Why is it, for someone who loves being in nature, finds it abhorrent to actually touch it?

She relents, surrendering to his soft entreaties. "Gosh! Tonight, you look so much like Harrison Ford," Halla comments.

"I do? Not clint Eastwood?"

"Well maybe Clint Eastwood too, but better looking. I get jealous. Women walking past, looking at you," she confides.

"You don't need to be. I am in love with you. I only have my eyes on you, Halla," he said.

Satisfied with his response, Halla lays back looking up into the universe where an occasional star shines through the night sky. "Amazing, so much sky. I would like to be a star one day."

"A movie star? said Calum.

"No, a star in the heavens shining back down to earth," she said, in a soulful tone.

"I think you could become a movie star far easier."

"Humm, we will see. When I become one, I will shine bright for you, so you always find me."

"Promise?"

"I promise. I want to be shining star for you."

"You can do anything," said Calum.

"You will always be able to find me. I make sure," her conviction is steadfast and resolute. A plan is building in her imagination. However, her aspiration demands a direct collaboration from the universe in order to deliver the promise to him, and to herself.

"That's interesting," said Calum. "Some Australian Aboriginal tribes believe the stars are the campfires of their ancestors. They are keeping them alight so they can find their way home."

For the first time in years, Halla feels she is able to move beyond her self-imposed limitations. Is it being in love that makes her feel this way? She wants to be the most authentic version of herself and to cultivate that same future for the one she desires by her side, Calum.

"With you, I feel I can do anything," she said, as she throws her arm across his chest forgetting for a moment the Korean culture of restrained demonstrations of public affection.

"It's getting dark. We should go," Calum said, as he nudged Halla.

"Yes, Are you hungry yet?" Halla replied.

"Not really. Are you?"

"Then let's go back to your hotel and after, I go home. Mongee and Songee will be wondering where I am."

Calum agrees, although he is taking a dislike to Halla's pets demanding so much of her time.

As they walk through the busy streets, Halla contemplates her role in their recent encounter with the elderly lady. What makes some people feel empathy more than others? Is it their environmental upbringing, a chemical imbalance or simply, their personality? The presence of Calum has changed her. She feels different with this new found sensation of feeling. How is this happening to her? Why is it happening? The answer floats away amongst the haste of the Friday night revellers, neon signs, restaurants and numerous karaoke night clubs.

"Today has been special for me, said Halla," as she tugs at Calum's arm. "I like this feeling between us," she added.

"Me too," replied Calum. "I am so happy to have you next to me again. You know you have become an event in my life. You are my latest drama," he added, not realising at the time, the full prophetic nature of his statement.

"Yes, it's like a car accident for me, a sudden impact."

"Oh, you mean like a collision?" he replied.

"Yes, I had a collision near the Han River. Life has never been the same. It's a wreckage." Halla laughed. "Why?" She continued.

"Why what?" said Calum.

"Why you come Korea?"

"Economics. It was the cheapest way to Canada from Thailand, via Korea."

Oh! You said, to meet me," Halla responded.

"Yes, and to meet you. More than anything, I came here to meet you."

"How long?" Halla continued.

"Three weeks. Which means our time is short," he replied.

"I don't want." said Halla as her heart sinks. "Not thinking about," she added, unable to disguise her disappointment.

Calum turns to Halla and says, "I am coming back for you."

"I want," said Halla, still absorbing the impact that his leaving will have upon her.

Mr 7.30 is in the distance walking toward them. Being vigilant, Halla sees him first. "Oh nice." Look it's him. Mr 7.30," smiles Halla. "He is funny," she adds.

"Halla! He is coming this way," replied Calum, hoping to avoid the chance encounter. "I don't want him to see me," said Calum, urging her into a dark alley out of view. "He will know I am back in Seoul and not staying with him."

"You are silly," responded Halla. "What does it matter?"

"I don't want him to think I didn't like his accommodation, that's all."

"Ok, we can hide here. Let's pretend we are lovers being naughty in the alley."

"I like that idea, but let's not pretend. Put your arms around me like this," Calum said, as he pulls her close.

They are in a position to have their first kiss, but Halla breaks their embrace, conscious of the crowded public street and that someone might be watching.

"I think he has gone. We can continue now," she said, pulling him back out on to the street.

"Oh, I was just starting to enjoy this," said Calum.

Halla's car is parked near Calum's accommodation with a note on the window which reads, *Please move*.

"Calum! I have to go. My car," said Halla.

"Oh," said Calum, searching for the words to change her mind. "You can have a shower here, if you like, after you find another car-park," realising it would not convince her to stay as soon as he said it.

"No. That is your shower. I have to go," she replied.

"We can both have one. I am sure they won't mind. That came out wrong.... I meant, not at the same time...I didn't mean that," laughed Calum.

Halla has a mental picture in her mind, one she will take home to bed with her that night. "Good night, Mr Calum with a C. I don't like you," said Halla.

"Good night, Miss Halla with a H. I don't like you either."

As she gets into her car, she looks at the pendent Calum had given her. She cradles it in her hand, bringing it close to her breast.

"Blue flowers. It is written, Calum. Everyone has a script to follow. So do we." With that, she drives off into the night.

Her words linger in the air, leaving Calum standing alone with the weight of another of her cryptic messages. Tethered to the enigma of that far-away look in her eyes, her words follow the sound of his footsteps to the emptiness of his room. He considers her fatalistic comment. It is woven with threads of destiny and yet, with the suggestion of a lack of free will, as though they are mere players on the cosmic stage directed by a supreme force. Calum wondered if the script she is referring to, could be rewritten, if the ink of fate is as indelible as the certainty of her statement.

The night held its secrets close. Into its soft embrace, he carries memories of the day they shared and fantasised of the dramatic story yet to unfold.

Chapter Thirteen

Calum often seeks solace through physical activity. It helps release negative thoughts that tenaciously cling to his spirit, a means of shedding all that has grown obsolete in his life.

Today he set off walking in the fresh morning air in an effort to clear his mind. As he moves, he visualises the past being swept off him, layer by layer. Redundant thoughts peel away, those that are no longer functional in his life. What remains, is fresh and new, free of residue, washed, as if by the relentless surf against a rocky outcrop.

Today, he aspires to cleanse not only the essence of his past but also, to release Halla's presence from his life. He is walking to clear his mind of her. She has been occupying his thoughts constantly since arriving in Korea. Now, he is determined to empty his mind of everything, including her. He needs to see the clarity of where this relationship is going, to get a better perspective, as he will be in Korea for only a short time. Then what? One of them will need to compromise for this romance to survive.

He has learned there are three elements to a relationship; lust, companionship and practicality, which hang under the umbrella of love. There is certainly an intense physical attraction being activated between them. They can talk and laugh together, her intelligence matching his. Their curiosity about the world allows them to converse for hours. But it is practicality that is the issue, he thought. He cannot afford to keep returning to her country. It is too expensive for him to live in Seoul. More importantly, they have diversely different personalities and personal needs. He must learn to separate to avoid getting himself into emotional trouble, that may lead to possible regret and loss.

Today unfolds differently. Weariness threatens to cloak him before he feels the weight of the past lift, the pathway to the future more clearly delineated. It is late morning already when he checks his map. He has completed a five-kilometre walk, however the pain in his left hip gnaws at him like a drill bit biting at his porous bones. The other thing that doesn't go according to plan is that, even though he convinced himself mentally he should move away from her, he finds he has walked her direction, unconsciously. The street is familiar, in fact it is the same one where she picked him up on the first day he had met her. He doesn't know exactly where she lives, but he knows he isn't far away from her home. She avoids giving him her address.

Mentally, he doesn't want to contact her, however, his fingers are being disobedient, sending her a text anyway.

Calum: Good morning.
Calum: I am out walking. So I can stop thinking about you.
Calum: But I am heading your direction.

Halla loves to sleep in late. 11.00am is the usual time she surfaces to meet the day. However, an annoying tinging sound on her phone wakes her from slumber earlier than usual. It hurts her ears.

"Is he crazy? she said. "It's so early." She curses the interruption.

Another text travels across the airwaves sending disturbing vibrations to her brain.

"Men!" she groans.

She turns her phone off. Then seconds later, unable to resist the temptation, turns it on again, just in case he calls.

Halla: Why you walk?
Halla: Where you now?
Calum: Not far from you. I wanted to save you the trouble coming to my place and finding a carpark.
Halla: Send me picture where you.

Calum senses she is upset. There wasn't any, 'good morning', 'nice to hear from you', messages. This leads him to wonder if he has called too early. He takes a photo, of some nearby distinctive landmarks, earthen mounds called the Mongchontoseong Earthen Fortification, which run through the suburb of Hanan for almost 3 kilometres.

After a considerable wait, Halla's car is once again beside him. Even the sound of her horn carries with it, her impatient mood. "Why you walk all the way here?" her voice, laced with frustration. "It's too far."

"So you would not have to find a car park," Calum replied, justifying his early morning calls with what he knew is a feeble excuse. He then slaps his wrist, labelling himself, "naughty kangaroo."

"Yes, naughty kangaroo. It's so early!" she added. There is no attempt to allow him to feel better, rather, adding to his guilt.

He redirects the conversation to food, which he hopes will sooth her temper. "Sorry to wake you. Let's get breakfast. I am shouting."

"Ok, I know a place. But first, I take you to hotel. You need shower. And, you don't need to shout. I can hear you."

"Shouting means, I am paying," Calum corrected.

"Oh. Thank you, my teacher" replied Halla. "I learn new word. Shooting."

"No, Shouting. Same word, multiple meanings. That's English for you."

Calum feels relief as her dark mood eases, having heard before, that if Asian women get angry, the suggestion of food will appease their disposition. The thought of sustenance distracts Halla, now that her appetite has returned.

"I have your washing here with me. You need change clothes."

No sooner had they found a park outside his hotel, there is someone waving them on.

"I am not going to say anything," said Calum, feeling vindicated from the charge of inappropriateness of calling earlier.

"Close your eyes, Miss Halla with a H." said Calum, as he enters his hotel room.

"No, I wait outside for you. Naughty Kangaroo."

Halla is outside the door for only a few minutes where, in the nearby kitchen, she finds some cleaning equipment. She is unable to resist tidying Calum's room. By the time she returns, he is already in the shower. The frosted screens are fogged further by the warm water. Surreptitiously, Halla peeks at Calum's body, making out his solid buttocks through the screen. It is that sight, the catalyst, which begins her mischievous intentions, an attempt to ensnare Calum in the enchantment of her carefully woven charms.

Halla has folded his washing. It is returned neatly presented, as though coming from a professional laundromat. Calum finds a pair of blue jean shorts, grateful for no longer having to wear long pants in the humid weather.

"My clean kangaroo," said Halla, with a pleasing smile as she sits down on the bed.

Little did Calum suspect that within the depths of her thoughts, a plan is evolving, a secret strategy, to satisfy her amusement but more so, the desire to explore the potency of her femininity.

"Halla! What are you doing!" cried Calum.

Halla has a cigarette lighter she is using to burn loose threads off his shorts. To Calum's shock and surprise, she is concentrating on the crotch area. Not that that is a particularly unusual thing to do, however, he happens to be wearing them at the same time.

"I am just making you tidy for when we go out for breakfast," said Halla, a coquettish smile adding to her mischievous intent. There is a subtle playfulness in her gaze, a silent invitation that speaks volumes as she kneels on her knees in front of him, her head at his waist height.

"Please be careful...Careful that you don't start a fire that the both of us are unable to put out," said Calum, unsuccessfully hiding his timorous feelings.

A prankish glint shines in her eyes, revealing the subtle thrill that tingles through her veins. This is not merely an act of caprice, it is a calculated exploration of the unspoken influence she holds, an acknowledgment of the enchanting power bestowed upon her by virtue of her womanhood.

Noticing a lump grow larger behind his zipper, Halla adds to his embarrassment. "Are you ok? You seem uncomfortable."

She wields her feminine prowess like a subtle enchantment, each gesture and glance imbued with the charm of her playful personality. Her plan unfolds successfully using the hypnotic influence nestled within the soft curves of her femininity and Calum, unwittingly drawn into the enchantment, becomes a willing participant.

Well, it's a bit hard to walk in public now you have done this to me." He is shocked she had initiated such a provocative challenge.

"A monster," whispered Halla.

Calum has found himself enchanted by the allure of beautiful women before, his resolve succumbing to the magnetic pull of their presence. This encounter, ignited by the flicker of a lighter, proves words are unnecessary in the burning language of desire. Her intentions resonate in that single flame. In this charged atmosphere, the potential of the moment envelopes him. The message is clear. He knows where this relationship is heading. It is not a question of if, but when. After her seductive performance, he knows it will be impossible to get her out of his mind, no matter how far he walks.

Spread across the breakfast table is an assortment of dishes surrounding a mixed rice bowl that includes vegetables, strips of seaweed, beef, topped with a fried egg. The dish is served with a spicy red pepper paste, called gochujang.

"This is called Bilimbap," said Halla. "Very popular. You should try a Dalgona coffee."

"I will, thank you," he replied, taking a sip. "This is yummy," said Calum, careful not to add any more colour to his already stained t-shirt. Much to his embarrassment, Calum notices Halla is able to get through a whole day looking perfectly neat and tidy, whereas he usually appears as though he has been in a food-fight by mid-morning.

"So, tell me Halla, you grew up here in Seoul. You must have seen a lot of changes since you were a little girl," Calum asked.

"Yes, a lot. I don't like change. I prefer everything to stay the same," her delivery is wishful, an acknowledgment of the impossibility of her statement. "I like order. When things are change, I no like. We are different in that way, you and me," she added.

"I don't like. Not, I no like," Calum corrected.

"You too! You no like?" said Halla.

"No, I am helping you with your pronunciation. The right way to say it is, I don't like, not, I no like."

"Oh, I don't like...I don't like you. That's right," she replied.

"I like order, but I am good with change. In fact, the opposite," he said, glancing off through the window. "Repetition is what unsettles me mostly," he added.

"At home everywhere." said Halla.

"But now, I am ready to drop the anchor. When I find the right person." he continued.

"Drop the anchor. I like that." she replied.

Halla is deep in thought wondering how the two of them can reconcile such obvious differences. Yet, there were signs presented to her impossible to ignore which connects her to him. Could she find a way for him to drop his anchor for her? she wonders.

"Halla, I have met your dog, but I would really like you to introduce me to your cat. What is her name?" he inquired, shielding a desire to see her domestic environment.

"Songee," responded Halla, careful not to give any indication he is about to receive an invitation to her home.

"Mongee and Songee. That's cute. I had a Siamese cat. But that was a long time ago, said Calum.

"What was its name?" she asked.

Calum hesitated at first, then he decides to take the risk. "I called her G-spot. G-spot the cat," replied Calum. He is curious if she knows the meaning of the word.

"G-spot! You called your cat, G-spot! That's sick," she laughed. I want to go home and stroke my G-spot," said Halla, hysterically. "I no like you Calum. Oh, I don't like."

The laughter they share is about to face a challenge that will test the resilience of their connection. Their bliss is on the cusp of an unforeseen twist, a turning point, the moment of revelation that will redefine the contours of their relationship.

"Are you feeling a little more relaxed now," said Halla with a cheeky smile.

Calum moves in his seat in readiness to take up a challenge. He interprets her question to be a subtle reference to their earlier interaction with the lighter. He suspects there is a competition about to start, a contest of innuendoes. They are both like duelling flamingos engaging in a verbal love dance on a daylight tryst. He is compelled to continue the seductive advance she initiated earlier. A flame was applied to his crotch, but his only immediate weapon, the power of activating her imagination through words.

"Yes Halla, I am still feeling the effect. Congratulations. You have made me feel like a...hungry lion."

The impact comes in the pronunciation, the slight pause, then the delivery of the last two words, a drop in octave down low and deep.

Oh, a hungry lion! That is how you feel now? A predator! Hungry for what?" she retaliates.

Calum's response is not measured or politically correct in any way. "In my imagination, I am a hungry lion circling around your bed. You are restrained, not physically. You are restrained by my hypnotic strength and power, with the expectation of what might be about to happen to you. You're aroused. Vulnerable. Waiting. I am a...hungry lion, wanting to lick you all over, hungry for you."

"Oh," replied Halla, unnerved by his masculine assertiveness, his blunt crude comment. She feels herself falling under the influence of both the confidence of his delivery as well as the sensuality the image inspires in her mind. The thought of a large tongue, hot and wet lashing against her nude body, between her legs, all over her, unstoppable and determined, is a provocative, tantalising concept.

Calum notices her moving in her seat and guesses she may be

feeling the effect of his delivery. His counter plan worked. Now they are on an equal playing field, at least, that is what he thinks.

Halla's eyes narrow, her demeanour, menacing and threatening. "That is so disrespectful! I am a lady, not some tramp you found in the park." With that, she abruptly gets up and leaves the restaurant with a stunned Calum, in hot pursuit. "Not in the script," Halla mumbles.

She is puffing away on her vape by the time he finds her, shifting her weight alternatively from one hip to the other like a boxer in readiness to defend a championship title. Their relationship, once filled with carefree laughter, now carries an undercurrent of tension. She is ready for a fight.

"So disrespectful!" said Halla, slapping him open-handed on the chest as he arrives. "I am a lady!"

"I'm sorry. Yes, you are a lady. I apologise," said Calum. He recognises a contradiction in her reaction. Such a volatile response to what he said, as compared to what she did with the lighter. He saw his comment, congruent and in context, but he admits, perhaps he was a little tasteless.

This is their first relationship challenge. Halla is in a turmoil of mixed emotions and bodily sensations. Calum is confused, unsure of how to reconcile the drama. They both struggle finding common ground.

"The lighter did it, Halla. It lit a fire in my mind and body that threw me into chaos. I'm sorry," said Calum, assigning her some of the blame for his paroxysm of eroticism, yet in his heart, he knows he is being unfairly treated. A double standard is being enacted, of which he feels he is the victim.

"And another thing, you cannot put your arm around me in public. We are only allowed hold hands. I let you do that because I care for your feelings. Naughty kangaroo!" she said, as she slaps him on the chest again. "Public demonstration of love is only for…not nice girls. It makes me look cheap. I know people here. I am a lady!"

"I am sorry. I didn't know," realising he is in more trouble because of his cultural ignorance. But now Halla is on her way back inside, moving with the determination of a Kamikaze pilot to the toilet. She is looking for release for her pent-up anger. Inside the bathroom, a mirror distracts her.

"Not need man," she cries. And then, with more determination. "Not need man!" She adopts an excessively feminine pose, while pretending Calum is standing beside her. "Not need man," punctuating her statement with a lady-like nudge, accompanied by a soft, tinkling giggle. Halla's character changes, taking a more aggressive stance. Her demeanour shifts into that of a strong, empowered woman. "Not need man!" This time her nudge is delivered with a definite forceful, aggressive push. The transformation continues, morphing into a martial-arts professional. "Not need man!" Two powerful Bruce-Lee-like Kung fu punches in quick succession with the final cat-meow to finish, directed at an imaginary Calum. "Moeoooougo!" Halla regains her composure just as rapidly. She adds final touches to her make-up, smiles charmingly, gives a lady-like giggle to her reflection in the mirror and returns to their table.

"Silly kangaroo!" said Halla. "Now I am angry."

"I am sorry," said Calum.

Halla sees evidence of his genuine remorse and begins to soften her attack. "Come on, we walk back to your hotel. I take you home. You spill food on your clothes again. Hungry lion. Come."

Calum is confused and disorientated, feeling as though all his energy has evaporated. "I am not feeling the best," said Calum. "Can I ask you to help me? I need to be around trees…nature, so I can ground myself."

"Sure, but am I the cause of how you feel?"

"No, not at all," he lied.

"Ok, I know place. We go."

The towering high-rise buildings in Busan as well as Seoul are starting to have an effect on Calum. Even with their architectural sophistication and beauty, they are making him feel small and claustrophobic. He needs to be next to nature, to feel the wind off the river. Now Halla has given him an unexpected mental challenge as well. She drives him to a park near the Han River.

"Thank you for bringing me here. It's what I need. And, to be with you. I feel better already," he added.

As they set off on a walk, Calum recovers quickly, becoming engaged in conversation with a group of tourists from California. He rarely has trouble finding people to chat with. Halla however, chose to keep walking. She sits on a seat a short distance away. This makes Calum uncomfortable. Why is she not joining him in the conversation? Is the residue of the hungry lion conversation still lingering? It isn't necessary for her to speak, just be by his side. He ends his chat with the tourists prematurely, in order to re-join her.

They are two different people. Calum is outgoing, friendly and comfortable with people. Halla, on the other hand, reserved, cautious and careful. But now, he can see she is also prone to sudden emotional volatility, something Calum has difficulty dealing with. These two almost opposite personality characteristics may become a burden for their relationship.

"Halla, I need to touch this tree to ground myself," said Calum, urging her to join him.

Halla reciprocates, in so doing, he suspects she is able to interact more easily with a passive species rather than a human being. He worries about this observation. He can't shake the thought that perhaps, in her past, she has weathered battles leaving scars on her soul, therefore shaping her into the enigmatic, reserved and yet, volatile woman he finds himself drawn to.

She presses up against the tree and in that moment, becomes entranced by its beauty. Rubbing the bark, she draws her ear closer, listening.

"Tree talk to me. Nature is alive everywhere. It communicates," she said, causing Calum's intrigue to rise.

"What did it say to you?" he asked.

"I am her. She is me," she whispers.

"What do you mean by that?" he replied, sensing her answer would be like holding the wind in his hands.

"I am her. She is me," she repeats her mantra without further qualification. "Excuse me, I have to make a call."

Halla moves away to make the call, just out of hearing range.

Calum cannot escape his yearning to understand the intricacies of her personality, to bridge the gap between the woman who walks beside him and the shadows that linger in the recesses of her past. It is a quick phone call. When she is finished, she returns to Calum.

"Is everything ok?" said Calum.

Halla is reluctant to answer. "Being artistic, as you say before, I have an appointment with my psychologist, every Wednesday. I needed to call them. I cancel to be with you."

"Oh, A psychologist? They have put you on anti-depressants?" asked Calum, surprised she volunteers the personal information.

"Yes, I take some. It helps me," she replied.

"Mind altering drugs, I call them," replied Calum. "I strongly disagree with using them.

Halla takes a defensive pose.

He continues. "They just stop us feeling. I prefer to experience all the emotions naturally. Tragedy, excitement, whatever comes my way. I don't know why they want to make us all feel happy, as though happiness is the only human feeling we are allowed. It's so one dimensional. Let's all be the same," he sighs.

"Yes, I suppose. I see your point, and I take sleeping pills," she added.

"Oh, too much. Not good for you. I wish you would stop. But that's up to you. It's just my uneducated opinion. But everyone needs someone to talk to. It's so hot. I am worn out. Can we go back?"

"Yes, it is *bery* hot," replied Halla, failing to pronounce *'very'* correctly.

"Oh, your pronunciation of that word, *very*, sounds a little Japanese," said Calum, as they walk back to the car.

Halla's persona shifts immediately. His comment, received like a slap in the face with a frozen fish. A repressed anger rises up from within her, the igniting of an old wound. "I not like that. Don't tell me I sound Japanese. Never! I hate."

"You hate Japanese. Why?" said Calum.

A resentment washes over her continence. "They try to take out country, our culture. Koreans were forced to worship at Japanese Shinto shrines, take Japanese names. Many Koreans, both men and women, forced to fight for Japan, work in mines, and factories. Never tell me I talk Japanese," she said. "Never!"

"I am sorry. I did not know people in Korea are still angry, but I can understand why," said Calum, his hand resting behind her shoulder in a show of support.

Her anger has not subsided. She moves away, turning the opposite direction. "The Japanese forced thousands of Korean women to provide sex for military."

"I did hear about that somewhere," replied Calum.

She turns to face Calum. "Somewhere! That somewhere is right here with my mother!" she replied, her finger pointing to the ground under her feet. "That is why...I not need men. I hope North Korea make nuclear on Japan." She hammers shut the topic with arms folded.

Calum did not know where to turn with his cultural misdemeanour. He has inadvertently stepped into a very sensitive area. Little did he know at the time, the brutality the Japanese inflicted upon Korean women prior to the end of World War 2, will reverberate down through the decades and soon, will have another major impact on him directly.

Chapter Fourteen

Halla does not like Calum's new accommodation. There is no air-conditioning. If she suddenly gets her hot flushes, there is nothing she can do, except leave, or have a cold shower. As they enter the room, it is airless and hot. As usual, Halla is in pursuit of a mirror making her way to the bathroom. She notices Calum had trimmed his beard leaving small strands of hair around the vanity. Placing them secretly in her handbag, Halla has a calculated plan. She believes these are a necessary component with which to ensnare him in a bond with her, a quest for permanent union.

Calum lays on the bed exhausted and overheated, dressed only in a pair of boxer shorts. Halla has a small towel which she wet, rubbing the coolness over his body.

"My Tarzan. You are so hot," her voice, a soothing balm to his troubled mind and body. Calum reciprocates, placing his finger on her leg, quickly pulling it away while making a 'shisss' sound. "You are hot too, my mystery lady."

As she rubs his body with the cool towel, she has another agenda on her mind. It is a hands-on exploration of his semi-nude male body, the wide shoulders, the sculpted muscles of his arms and the firm legs. She follows the currents of his chest hair as though directed by a gentle breeze. It's been a long time since there has been this opportunity to get close to a man. Only in her imagination, does she have this experience. After she finishes, she sits beside him.

"Beautiful man, said Halla, as she holds her gaze with his. "They have the sea in them, your eyes. Blue skies. Blue eyes. Like my go mingo."

"Your cat? She is Siamese?" Calum asks. "Like my G-spot".

"Yes. Blue eyes, like you."

"Beautiful lady. Thank you. I feel so much cooler," Calum sighs with relief.

Halla threw a glance his way. "I am sorry about today, Calum."

"I forgive you. I like you when you are angry. It's really ok." Calum grabs her hand. "I was out of line."

Halla continues. "I get angry sometimes. I not explain. I cannot manage my mood...my life." a regretful crease etches across her forehead.

"Don't go home. Stay with me," he pleads.

"I have to go. My dog. My cat waiting for me. They get anxious without me," a sad whisper in her voice as she lays on her back across Calum's waist, her head and shoulders resting against the adjacent wall. This is causing him some concern, as almost certainly, she will feel his passion rise beneath her. She is making herself prone, inviting Calum to lay his hands on her. He wonders if he should participate, in light of the confusing events of the day. He refrains, opting to hold her hand instead. "You have callouses. What's that from?"

"Dog grooming," she replied, pulling her fingers away. It won't go away." Halla keeps her OCD behaviour to herself. Calum finds it hard to believe that dog-grooming would cause callous on the tips of her fingers. Instead of challenging her, he chose to let her think she has convinced him.

She sits up, her elbow near his groin. He is being invited down another seductive pathway, her arm occasionally bumping a lump that is forming in his shorts. He is conscious of her playful secretive movements. She must be aware of what she is doing. Their dopamine levels are elevating. A conscious unspoken communication is underway once again, but Calum questions if he is getting the right signals, being reluctant to participate after the previous reactions.

"Bring them here. Your pets," Calum said, although he knows what the answer to his suggestion will be.

"To meet G-spot? Great idea. I would like to introduce my pets to your G-spot," she laughs. You are so....I no like...I don't...like you."

"I would love to introduce you..." Calum stops himself, unwilling to experience another display of hostile emotional reaction.

Calum surmises that perhaps she is a reclusive type at heart, preferring solitude and the company of her pets, and he, adding a complexity to her life.

"Halla, I have to ask. Are you feeling good being around me?"

"Fine, I like. You are fun to be with...sometimes, not all the time," she replied.

"I am worried I am causing you conflict, me being culturally insensitive, among other things."

"We will be Ok. Everybody has a story to follow. Tomorrow, I have a surprise for you. I want to take you driving into the country," said Halla.

"Away from the city? Nice. Where are we going?"

"Somewhere interesting. It's a surprise. I blindfold you."

"Seriously! Blindfolded? Oh my god, sounds exciting," said Calum, unable to contain his enthusiasm. "Where on earth did you come from?" Calum jokes.

"You met me after coming to Korea and asking me if I would like a coffee. That's where I came from," she replied.

"Really, is that what went wrong, I knew I took a wrong turn somewhere." She smacks him lightly and turns away. "Really, you can blame Mongee for us getting together. She pulled me in the direction of the river to meet you, both times."

"That naughty Mongee. I need to talk with her," said Calum.

"Good night, Calum. Mr Calum with a C." Halla leans over and kisses him on the hand. "I will be back here early at 10.00am tomorrow. I text you when I'm on the way."

Before Halla leaves his room, she moves to the window overlooking the street below. She surveys the area surreptitiously, before disappearing down the hall leaving Calum to question the events of the day. He wonders if Halla has mental health issues which may cause conflict in their relationship. The next day might remove all doubt.

Chapter Fifteen

Halla: I am coming

Calum: Here waiting.

Halla: We must change phone numbers. We are being tapped.

Calum: What! Tapped! Scammers?

Halla: I think so.

Upon entering his hotel room, Halla is quick to retrieve Calum's mobile. "My number changed. Now, I change you phone. New sim card," said Halla.

"I have checked. They didn't take anything?' said Calum.

"Best to be safe. All fixed. Now we go," said Halla, urging him out of the room. "My car is near," she added, as they go down the stairs to enter her vehicle.

"Ok Halla, It's you and me, together again. Take me away," smiled Calum, as they drive off to the east coast of Korea.

Halla reaches her hand across, squeezes Calum's arm and slides down to hold his hand. "Yes, you and me together."

"Hey, where is the blindfold you promised?" said Calum.

"Not yet. I want you see the country scenery first. It's about a 3-hour drive. Near the end, I blindfold you. I cannot wait."

"Halla, tell me more about your name, the meaning of it. I am interested in learning everything about you," Calum asked.

"My name? Ok, you remember Valhalla, the Norwegian kingdom in heaven?"

"Yes, I remember that bit," he replied.

"And that my parents intended to live in Norway?" Halla continues with reluctance. "Well, my father wanted to call me.... it's a bit embarrassing for me."

"Go on, I won't tell anyone. It's our secret," replied Calum, zipping his lips with his fingers for added emphasis.

"He wanted to call me...Val, as first name, with middle name, Halla, therefore, Val-Halla. My mother would not agree. Thank you, Mom," as she motions toward the heavens.

"I love that story. I really do. I appreciate you sharing," said Calum, reaching across and putting his hand on her leg, to which she responds by placing her hand over his. "Can you take me to Valhalla?" he added.

"Yes, I will. But not today." She replied. I promise. Today, I have somewhere else I want to show you."

"I am really happy you are doing the speed limit today," said Calum, reminding her of his discomfort at driving too fast.

"Ok, it's boring, but I will," she returns his smile. His comment, encouraging her to check in the rear-view mirror in case they are being followed.

The tour across Korea takes them on a four-lane drive through beautiful mountainous scenery and numerous tunnels to eventually arrive in the vicinity of Halla's secret destination.

"Are we here already?" asked Calum.

"Not yet. This is where you stop sightseeing. I have red scarf. Tell me if you see through."

"Ok, I promise." Calum responded.

"What are you expecting to see? I am curious," she said, as she begins blindfolding him.

"Let's see...A waterfall?"

"No."

"The ocean?"

"Uah ha, not the ocean. Maybe in the background," she said, amused by his wild guesses.

"Perhaps some beautiful Korean women with fans doing a seductive dance," Calum teased.

"Naughty kangaroo." She slaps him lightly on the leg.

Halla drives for another five minutes and enters a carpark. She assists him out of the vehicle.

"Be careful. We are nearly there.," she said.

"I cannot see a thing and I cannot see you."

"Really, that's a surprise. I wonder why," said Halla, laughing while leading him by the hand. "Ok, stop here. You know how you like to hug trees. Well, this is a hugging rock. Put your arms around and kiss. I take picture."

"Ok, I will play along. It's big...and cold." he said, feeling a large sculpted stone object before him.

"Yes big," laughed Halla as she takes a photo. "A monster," she mumbles under her breath. "You are funny. Now you can take your blindfold off. Tell me what your shock value score is out of ten," she added.

Calum pulls the red scarf off, however, he wishes he hadn't, as the sight totally catches him off guard. He has kissed and hugged a giant penis sculpture.

"What! Halla! This is terrible! Give me that camera," said Calum, as he chases after her.

"Ok, I delete. Shock value?" she persists.

"Ten out of ten. Definitely! What is this place? It's freaky," said Calum. Surveying the area, he sees approximately 50 statues, depictions of the human penis exhibited in various sizes and styles.

"It's called Samcheok park. This is where we have the Penis Culture Festival."

"You got me, big time Halla. I won't forget this...ever. So many!"

"It is the location where a virgin girl died. You might want to sit and rest," said Halla, urging him toward a seat which has male genitalia carved in the base. As she sits down, it is directly between her legs.

"I am not going to sit there! Not ever!"

"Oh, come on Calum, it won't bite you. "It doesn't have teeth."

"No man in his right mind would sit there. Get off! You are making me jealous," he protests, as he pulls her off the seat. "Oh my God! What a place! There is nothing like this in Australia."

"Come on, there is more to see and the day is getting small."

"The day is getting small," Calum repeated. "I like that. Can I use that one?"

"Sure."

"Can I keep you. You are so much fun...sometimes," said Calum.

"I want," said Halla, as she kisses his hand.

"The day is getting small," whispered Calum.

"Come, I have another surprise for you," she said, inviting Calum to follow. "It's a short drive from here."

As they travel off to the next location, he reconsiders his previous opinion of the reserved, sexually repressed Korean culture from his observation of people swimming fully clothed in Busan. The explicit examples of phallic symbols, proves to him, Korea is a land of contradictions, and his new found friend, equally so.

"We are in Bangye–ri. This is where the oldest most beautiful tree in Korea is," says Halla, proud of her unique heritage. "Three hundred million years. The Gingko tree. We must be careful. A legend says a white snake lives in this tree."

"A white snake. I am lucky to have a guide like you," said Calum, thinking the whole trip is a never-ending day of phallic symbols.

Halla carefully selects seeds from under the tree, kissing each one individually while placing them in a bag. In a low voice, she recites an invocation.

"Warm seed, love run strong; warm heart, let us never part," she chants.

"What did you say?" asked Calum.

"It's a love vow. You can say with me."

Calum repeats her words. "Warm seed...Love run strong. Warm heart. Let us never part."

"Where is the white snake? I cannot see it," said Calum, surveying the upper branches.

"You need to look with your third eye. It take practice. Kangaroo! Look! On that branch. He is looking at us. Be careful!"

"No, I still can't see it. Are you sure you are not imagining things."

"The white snake appears when the searcher is ready, not before," she explains.

"The searcher?"

Halla went on to qualify. "The searcher is the one who wants to see, beyond the wall. Hidden things. Magic and mystery. The one who sacrifices." her eyes, glazed and distant.

"Tell me, Halla," said Calum, shocked by this sudden revelation. "You can see the snake. Have you seen other...hidden things?"

"Calum, I am a Korean Shaman," she confides, as the burden of truth is lifted from her. "What? You look surprised," she adds.

"Halla, you surprise me every day," replied Calum.

"Because I not dress like one, does not mean, I am not. Sharman can look normal person. Not necessary dress like one. Most Sharman had near death experience.

"Have you?"

"Yes," Halla pauses, but refuses to elaborate. She has a cupped hand full of seeds from the Gingko tree which she studies as though looking into a crystal ball.

"What do you see?" Calum asked.

"I see the hand that guides, I see us together...until the time... when it becomes small."

"I am not sure what to say." Calum responds. That's why I call you my mystery lady. My multi-dimensional mystery."

"Come, my teacher, gu gu. gar gar. That means, let's go back now. I take home and roast. They are nice to eat. Not nice to smell." She holds her nose and makes a face to Calum.

"Ok yes, the day is getting small," he replied.

Calum can't help but marvel at the twists and turns life has taken leading him to Halla, the strangest lady he has ever met. He realizes that sometimes, the most beautiful moments emerge from the depths of uncertainty and spontaneity. She has given him that in no uncertain terms. The doubts that have clouded his mind earlier now seem trivial in comparison to the overwhelming sense of amazement he feels for her. The layers she presents are unending. However, that feeling of connectedness, only temporary, for Halla is a changeable character, one minute warm and loving, the next, aloof and distant. He compares her to an ice-cold artic storm blowing across a hot desert plain, spreading snow upon the shifting dunes one day, and then, without warning, a raging fire storm of love and lust the next.

Upon their return to Seoul, Halla takes him to a restaurant specialising in Bulgogi, a style of Korean Beef Barbecue.

"Are you enjoying your meal? You can add some flavour or, perhaps these might appeal," she said, offering him a bowl of bright red chillies.

"Yes, I like chillies, but not too hot."

"Do you? Did you know the Korean word for chili, is, gochu?" She smiles. Another well-laid trap is being prepared for her unsuspecting friend.

"I like gochu," said Calum, innocently adding some to his meal.

"Really, you like gochu? That's funny. It is the same word for penis in Korean," she laughs.

"What! That's not true," replied Calum.

"Yes, it is." she said, carefully choosing a large chilli with her chop sticks, raising it to her lips, licking it suggestively. She waits for a response from Calum. It doesn't take long.

"Halla! Stop that!"

"What? I like chillies. No, I looovve gochu," she said, laughing at his embarrassed expression.

"I not like. I not need chilli. Not need women," said Calum, with a disgusted expression. "You got me twice today."

"I not need men," she retorts.

"Is that true? Really. I think you do." Calum questions her conviction.

"No! Absolutely not!"

"You seem to hang around me often. I happen to be a man."

"I like you a little bit. Not love you ...maybe a little bit. Remember we are friends." she continues.

"You know it's women who choose the man generally," Calum

said. "Yes, men chase the woman, but the woman decides if she is going to slow down enough for him to catch her."

"You think that? she questions his observation. "We are friends remember. I am *4B* woman. The third part. No! A refusal to heterosexual marriage."

"A 4B woman? What about your natural physical desires? You cannot deny them. Feminine urges. You made me chase you and there is a lot of fun in the chase." Men are designed for it."

"For many years, I cut my hair and dressed as a man, to avoid relationships...people," she confides.

"I think I like you as a woman better," replied Calum, dismissing her statement as though it is an attempt at humour. However, for Halla, it isn't meant to be funny. It comes from a need to confide, to share a lifestyle forced by circumstance.

Calum is slurring again and talking fast, so excited about his own conversation, he has virtually forgotten Halla is in the restaurant. She isn't happy about that.

Calum continues rambling. "You know men just want one thing. They want to diversify the gene pool. That's what an anthropologist said. I saw it on the internet and that theory holds some weight. It's in our design. That's how we are made, by the universe."

"Where does love come into that?" remarks Halla, not enjoying the conversation. Conflicting thoughts are occupying her mind now, her resolve to live free of intimate relationships and her desire to connect with Calum on a soul level.

"Good point. Where does love come into that? Perhaps we are more than our primal urges," replied Calum, deep in contemplative thought.

"Calum! Calum! You are talking too fast. I cannot understand you. Slow down," said Halla, hoping to end the topic.

It's then Calum has a realization. He is able to have an enjoyable conversation on his own. He doesn't need anyone else. He can be a pack animal and a lone wolf at the same time. Halla is proof. She doesn't understand most of what he is saying.

"Oh sorry...I got a bit carried away," said Calum.

"Oh, my phone. It must be the bat-te-ly," she complains.

"The what?"

"Bat-er-ly," she repeats.

Calum is struggling to understand what she means. The more she says the word, *battery*, the more it becomes impossible for him to interpret.

"Bat-er-ly! Bat-er-ly Bat-er-ly! Bat-er-ly Bat-er-ly! Bat-er-ly. You don't understand? Bat-er-ly! Bat-er-ly," Halla points to her mobile phone, frustration raising within.

The clanging sounds coming from the kitchen, people talking loudly in the restaurant, together with the alcohol, does not help Calum comprehend what she is saying.

"I am sorry, I am trying...." But Calum is cut off.

"I good at English. What wrong with you?" She makes a face at him, similar to the one she makes at her dog, as if Calum has suddenly turned into a pile of dog shit on her nice clean quilt.

Does she have to turn this into a scene as well? Calum thinks to himself. Do I need this roller coaster ride?

"Bat-er-ly! Bat-er-ly! Bat-er-ly! Bat-er-ly! She repeats. Her eyes, once kind and loving, now hold a fiery storm, untamed and angry. For Calum, the intensity of her reaction surpasses the boundaries of reason and logic.

"Oh, I get it. Battery," said Calum.

"Oh, you get it, do you! Excuse me," with that, she stomps out of the restaurant, a swirling mass of anger following. This time, Calum remains where he is with the gamble of perhaps, never seeing her again.

For Halla, the conversation was a challenge, an objectification of her gender. The internal conflict of her confusion about being with him manifests into the hostile reaction. He neglected her attempt to discuss why she avoided relationships for many years. As a result, she feels dismissed.

Calum can see something in her eyes he has never noticed before. There is a certain wild contempt that is unfounded. Was the topic about diversifying the gene pool too confronting for her? He saw their discussion as a means to engage in a philosophical conversation. The reaction was disproportionate to how someone should respond ordinarily to a similar situation. Yet, he is emotionally involved, his judgement clouded by feelings. He is out of his depth when it comes to severe emotional mental problems, he thought.

He wonders if he can continue to navigate the twists and turns of her erratic mind. Is it possible for him to ride these volatile ups-and-downs and survive? Is love, the panacea for all tribulations, now posing its own dilemma. The depths of her frequent internal mental distress, hinted at a terrain unfamiliar to Calum.

He questions if the power of love, a force he once believed boundless, can surmount this uncharted emotional landscape. So does she.

Chapter Sixteen

A morning excursion proves to be a wonderful experience together, once they apologised to each other. Lunch across the Han River put them in a jovial, playful mood. But then, because of the actions of the North Korean Government, the day turned into a confrontation for both of them.

The sound of the presidential alert warning everyone to find refuge on the subway still clings to Halla's memory. Now she is worried the romantic elixir given to Calum before she left his hotel will prove to be an even bigger challenge for him. However, she knows it is designed to be an initiation, a catalyst, to help him become conscious of the spiritual realms alongside her. She wants to contact him, to speak of the difficulty she is experiencing being in a relationship after so many years, to apologise for leaving him alone in the room. The challenges she faces sometimes seems insurmountable, yet her conviction overrides her uncertainty. Instead of calling, she places her trust in the magic of her potent brew, recognising the process should take its course during the night, uninterrupted.

Calum is caught in the web, the drama of love, a challenging and intoxicating substance, so intensely addictive, it becomes difficult to stop the self-sacrifice and emotional torture. As the night wears on, his vision of meeting Halla becomes increasingly vivid. Her concoction is entering his blood system, the chemical effect, beginning to take hold. In a hypnagogic state, between being awake and asleep, Calum becomes aware the environment of his hotel room is changing dramatically.

The bedside lamp flickers rapidly as the ceiling fan stops. It reverses direction, spinning at high speed. The room fills with snowflakes. They fall from the ceiling as the room temperature becomes ice cold, pushing back the relentless Korean humidity. They transform from snowflakes into stardust, a prelude to a supernatural event. Two metallic darts fly through the air in his direction. They are the piercing eyes of a black cat staring through him. It leaps into the air capturing a pink butterfly, then escapes out the window, not before savaging it to death.

Then everything stops. The fan vanishes. The lights extinguish. Iridescent stardust falls from a vast blackness above. A low humming sound begins of Buddhist prayer bowls. It is then, she arrives. Halla is back in his hotel room. There is something extraordinarily different about her.

Halla, is now a Korean Goddess, commanding attention with every step. Gone is the uncertainty; in its place, a woman transformed, radiating confidence and determination. She moves with grace, holding the promise of whispered desires. The atmosphere pulses with an otherworldly energy. A vision of ethereal beauty makes her entrance.

Her glossy black hair flows like a river of midnight silk, cascading over her shoulders, framing her firm, round breasts. Her eyes, dark and piercing, reveal a newfound intensity, a reflection of her unwavering resolve. As if drawn by an irresistible force, more butterflies in hues of pink and blue fly around her head, creating an orbiting halo accentuating the gravitational pull of her exquisite allure. Adorned in golden ornaments gleaming in a soft glow of radiant stardust light, a sapphire necklace hangs suspended between her breasts, drawing attention to the charisma emanating from her presence.

A seductive dance begins. Two traditional Korean fans, glowing bright and shiny, the colours of peacock feathers, flash in time with her erotic sway. A white tiger, majestic and protective, flanks her, his low growl accentuated by an intense hungry gaze, resonating with power, untamed, threatening.

The room bows to her presence, as if acknowledging the arrival of a celestial being. In the swirling mystery surrounding her, a fire burns bright from within her breast, its warmth permeating the air, enveloping the entire space. The essence of passion and desire is taking tangible form with Calum, mesmerised by the scene unfolding.

She spoke, her voice, a soft and melodic symphony, like the gentle rustle of leaves in a summer breeze. "I am her. She is me," she said. "It is forbidden for you to look upon me."

With that, Calum is compelled to turn away, commanded by a divine authority and in that moment, he enters sleep paralysis. Immobilised, he is at her mercy, powerless to resist her captivating advance. "I want," she purrs. He hears her moan as the weight of her warm moisture envelops his manhood. Never before has he experienced this level of firmness, as though all his blood and vitality has rushed to a single point, his phallus. His very existence is no more than an erect penis, feeling the beat of his heart within. It is engulfed by a celestial being and the energy of her fire upon him, about to be launched by the lure of a seductive goddess. She screams, as he explodes. They catapult into space, to the stars and beyond. The exquisite marvel of the universe holds them close and connected, cocooned in all its spender and glory, but then, she is gone.

With a thud, Calum returns to reality. All that remains is the fall of the iridescent sparkle of stardust transforming again into snowflakes. It too, vanishes. He is spent, exhausted and empty. Rapidly, he falls back into the ordinariness of the hotel room, returning swiftly into another fantasy realm, that of sleep.

A sweet, evocative memory is all that remains of the encounter.

Chapter Seventeen

Next day, Calum is walking again. The residue of the threats of nuclear destruction still with him. The experience of the night imprinted on his soul forever.

Who is the woman who swept into his room and took him to the stars? That is the question he needs to unravel, the experience affecting him profoundly. It was so real, an unforgettable, spiritual encounter. He needs to know her true identity. Even though she has the appearance of Halla, her powerful energy is completely different to the woman he knows. The one who visited him in the night, tangible, but definitely otherworldly.

There is no other recourse than to explore the recesses of his memory, retracing the research done previously on female deities from ancient history. This is a work in progress as part of his plan to write his next book, an exploration of patriarchal and matriarchal societies. Perhaps the puzzle will become clear from this investigation, he thought.

Halla: Where are you now?

He has studied the legend of Sophia, meaning 'wisdom' from Gnosticism. She is a feminine figure, analogous to the human soul but also, one of the feminine aspects of God. Gnostics believe that she is the syzygy, the female twin of Jesus. In the Nag Hammadi texts, she is an anthropic expression of the emanation of the light of God, the fallen Goddess.

The story of Ruha, from the obscure religion, known as Mandaeism, parallels the Gnostic story of Sophia, falling out of the pleroma, the totality of divine powers. Ruha first dwells in the World of Light, until she 'falls' and bears a son.

He turned to his understanding of the Seraph, his obsession unrelenting. Seraph, a Jewish Celestial Being is placed fifth within the ten ranks of the angels in the hierarchy. In the Kabbalah, the Seraphim are the higher angels of the world of creation.

Calum's research had uncovered the fallen goddess legend, repeated in many belief systems. A reoccurring theme, descending to earth, invariably, falling in love with a mortal. He decides to keep his ego in check. What would a true goddess of the spiritual realms want with him, not having any redeeming qualities?

Nonetheless, the search moves on. In the pursuit of truth, clues to her identity, he feels goose bumps with a sudden realisation. No one fits her description more accurately than the mythological female demon called, Succubus, a creature from a parallel universe who desires intercourse with men. She derives her energy and sustenance from the primal creative force of life, the semen of men.

In that moment, Halla returns to the forefront of his mind. Earlier, she introduced him to the legend of Jacheongbi, the feminine deity, ruling love and sacrifice. This thought process provokes another profound and confronting question on his quest for an answer. Is Halla much more than a Sharman? Could she really be the fallen Korean goddess, Jacheongbi? He remembers she had told him how she secretly disguised herself as a man for many years. This is identical to the myth of the goddess, Jacheongbi, who did the same. According to legend, she descended to earth and fell in love with a mortal.

Calum ponders if Halla has been dropping hints as to her true identity ever since he first met her, waiting for him to connect the dots. Is that what she means, "I am her. She is me." He is compelled to decipher other clues laid out like cryptic signposts. How else should he interpret her comment made early in their relationship, when she said, 'Perhaps you will meet her while in Korea. But will you recognise?'

Is she a double agent, masquerading by day as an ordinary Korean woman, yet by night, transforms into a mythological celestial creature from beyond the spectrum of 3-dimensional reality. He wonders, is it possible to span two worlds at will, the celestial domain, with that of mortals who inhabit earth?

But then, another atrocious thought crosses his mind, one that heightens his suspicions even more. Is she playing with his mind out of some macabre amusement, twisting his sense of reality?

Halla: Answer me!...please. I am worried.
Calum: I am walking.

For the first time since meeting her, he feels uncomfortable, unsure if he wants to be in her presence so soon.

Halla: Where are you. Tell me!

He relents.

Calum: I am walking through Olympic Park, trying to clear my mind again.

Halla is concerned. He feels distant. Is he upset that she left so quickly the night before? Is he expecting more from her? Was the love potion too strong for him?

Halla: Send me a picture of where you are. I am driving to you.

Calum wants personal space to consolidate his thought processes, but she is insistent. He finds a cafe nearby, forwarding her a picture of the menu with the name of the restaurant displayed prominently.

Halla: Send picture of the outside.

There are only two cafes in Olympic Park. Surely, she can recognise the name from the photo he had already sent, he thought. They had been there together earlier in their relationship. Another image arrives on Halla's phone.

Halla: Is there a reason why you not show the name?

He suspects there is a demon after him, impossible to please. Regardless, off goes another image.

Calum: I wait for you here.

Calum waits in the cafe for her to arrive. Halla enters, sitting silently at the rear of him, out of his peripheral range. She is quiet, observing him from behind. It isn't until he glances around, that he sees she has arrived.

"Oh, there you are," said Calum, wondering why she didn't come straight to him upon arrival. She could not have missed him. He is the only one at that end of the restaurant.

"Why you walk? Walk! Walk! Walk! Everywhere!" said Halla, demanding an answer, while presenting him with a scowling look.

Calum chose a measured response. "It was a big day yesterday. I wanted to clear my mind."

"Of me? You want to forget about me?" Halla's delivery, short and sharp. Her voice cuts the air.

"No, of course not. It was a big night too, after you left," Calum explains. "I had a dream. A very vivid one. I am still processing it."

"Can we get coffee and go?" said Halla.

Calum is annoyed. Generally, people like to hear about another person's dream or, polite enough to listen. She shut the conversation down like the fall of a guillotine, making him increasingly suspicious.

"Sure." he replied.

Her mood softens.

"You seem different today, Calum. Are you Ok? Do you still love me?" said Halla, as she pulls his arm closer. "I'm sorry, about last night."

He began to question her sanity, as well as his own. He loves the lady walking beside him, but what is she hiding? This is not the first time he has seen a dark mood descend on her, only to change, just as rapidly.

"I love you a lot. I don't like you at the moment," replied Calum. "Just a little preoccupied."

He feels he needs to work his way through his current suspicious mind frame. Perhaps, the memory of the dream will wear off throughout the day, giving him a clearer perspective.

"Let's get drunk tonight, me and you," said Halla, as they wander toward her car.

"Ok, our time is short....small," Calum replied. "I really want to know you more, who you really are, down deep inside."

"You want to know me more? Everything?" she gives him an intense, unnerving gaze.

"Yes, everything. The truth," Calum said.

"The truth? About me? First you must find the truth of who you are," she said, looking directly into his eyes. "Yes, let's dance and sing our way through the night. Me and my Kangaroo," she adds. "Your eyes! They look so bright."

"My eyes?" Calum replied. "Perhaps they have been opened, last night." He chose to play along with what he now suspects, is a charade.

Halla could see subtle physiological changes in Calum. His arms look stronger. He seems taller, older and his eyes, more hypnotic than ever. Like a scientist watching the results of her experiment, Halla makes mental notes. She is aware of Calum's emotional distance, realising there is work to do to lure him back into her web. "I will make him love me," she whispers to herself.

"You look so handsome today, my kangaroo." Halla puts her hand on his leg placing her fingers a short distance under his shorts. Calum succumbs rapidly, responding by putting his fingers in the tears in her jeans. "Thank you. You are like a shining light to me. Can I keep you?"

"Yes, you can," Halla replied, throwing him a seductive glance, surprised at the rapid effectiveness of her plan.

As the day progresses and the memory of the night fades, Calum chastises himself for thinking ill of her. Even if she is a Succubus, is that so bad, he thought. If she is the goddess of myth and legend, even better. He entertained the idea of a repeat performance from the previous night. He is in want of more.

Calum!! Calum!! Come back. Come back to earth!"

"Huh," replied Calum, as he returns from contemplation of his dream from the previous night.

"I find new hotel for you," Halla continues. "It's bigger and not expensive."

"A new hotel. Good idea. I cannot wait to see it. Let's concentrate on having a good time today, to make up for yesterday." Calum replied.

They park the car at Halla's friend's place, a kilometre from Gandong shopping and entertainment district.

"I will park here, at my friend's place. We can walk," said Halla. "It is hard to find a place to put car."

"Sure, that makes sense, replied Calum. Let's find a bar and start the night off," he added.

Calum and Halla walk to an entertainment precinct that has numerous restaurants and bars. The heat of the afternoon sun is bearing down on them. Halla is conscious of the likely effect it will have on her. She is also aware that Calum seems to have forgotten about her condition.

"What do you think of this one?" said Calum.

Halla doesn't respond. After several different suggestions, it is she who is now becoming distant and silent. "Are you ok?" Calum inquired.

"You just think of yourself. Not me...ever," she snaps.

Calum is caught off guard, the delivery and tone hits like a freight train. "What?" says Calum in amazement. "Where is this reaction coming from all of a sudden?"

Halla doesn't answer. Instead, she stops still with her arms folded, seething with anger. Calum cannot understand its origin. "What's the matter? I thought we agreed we were going out to have a drink and a good time."

"Never me, always you. I am hungry. You not think of me. Never me." she scolds.

Calum finds an alternative suggestion in an attempt to diffuse the sudden hostility that has taken hold of her. "Alright, let's find a place where we can eat and have a drink at the same place. I don't have a problem with that."

The idea seems to bring a slight ease to her mood, although the tension lingers.

They stroll through the dimly lit streets, together yet apart, searching for a place that will serve both their appetite and quench a thirst. Halla is ever mindful of potential threats in the passing crowd. Finally, they stumble upon a charming restaurant, its ambiance inviting them in with a menu that promises both delectable dishes and a variety of alcoholic beverages. A large plate of succulent chicken materializes, accompanied by a generous serving of spices and flavourings. The soju makes its usual appearance. Perhaps this will be the bridge to mend the widening gap between them, Calum thought.

However, Halla's bad mood lingers like a storm cloud, refusing to dissipate.

"It's always you. What you want. I am hungry! You never think of me...ever," her accusation, bashing through the air like a blunt hammer.

"That's not true. I am always thinking of you," he pleads in his defence, his face reflecting a mix of hurt and confusion.

But Halla is relentless, her hostility unabated. "Liar!" she spat, her tone cold and merciless, eyes dark with anger. This comment hits Calum even harder. Another crushing blow, a false, unnecessary and baseless charge. An emotional drama such as this, he had not predicted, nor desires in his life.

"Excuse me," he responds, not willing to prolong the confrontation. Calum wants to be away from her presence, out of range of further attack. Being a moving target seems the safest option in the midst of such emotional turmoil. He lit a cigarette outside as he questions why he is allowing himself to be put through this vicious, emotional minefield. It was a direct impact to the heart.

Left alone in the restaurant, Halla is forced to consider the aftermath of her outburst. Uncertain whether Calum has abandoned her permanently and retreated to the hotel, she feels a pang of regret. Realizing the impact of her anger, she gathers her composure and searches for him outside the restaurant. Yet it is he, that finds her.

Calum is not holding back on hiding his displeasure. "I thought the idea is we are to have fun tonight. I don't like you at all at the moment."

"Sorry," she said.

"Liar? What is this bullshit, he retaliates. I don't know why you would say that. That is the worst insult possible."

"I am sorry," Halla said, trying to redeem herself. "I have anger management issues," she continues, confessing a vulnerability that lay beneath her usually controlled exterior. It is a plea for understanding and a hopeful pathway back to the warmth that had drawn them together in the first place.

"I don't like you at all, but I have this problem. I love you," Being magnanimous by nature, a sudden rush of forgiveness overcomes Calum. He recognises she has emotional problems and that he should take that into account. If his love is true, then should he not accept her for who she is, no matter the challenge.

"My kangaroo loves me," Halla said. "Let's go back in and celebrate. The Makgeolli is waiting for us.

Halla is holding her liquor a lot better than Calum. In fact, he is starting to make a nuisance of himself with the staff, as well, embarrassing Halla. At the end of the table, buzzers are positioned, used to call waiters to the table. Calum is aware of them, but he constantly bumps them accidently, setting off a call to their table. At first, it is amusing, however the staff find it too annoying, eventually removing them to silence the false alarms.

"You drink too fast, Slow down. Soju is very strong," Halla advised.

As the night progresses, he is only just able to stand, needing the assistance of Halla to make it back to the hotel. Fortunately, it is only a short wobble away.

"You know I want to keep you.... and take you... home with me... my mysterious princess, my...goddess," said Calum, surprised he managed to stumble through a full sentence.

"Sure," said Halla, knowing the promise of someone inebriated carries little weight.

Upon entering the hotel room, Halla removes his shoes. Bending over for Calum, is way beyond his capacity. He falls into bed. "Are you staying with me? Are you coming again tonight?" slurred Calum.

"Is who coming?" quizzed Halla.

"The lady who was here last night...the goddess with the pet tiger," he continued.

"Pet tiger? What pet tiger?" she repeats, finding the conversation slightly amusing.

"I know. Stay with me again. It's ok, Halla. I know the truth." That is the last audible words that parts his lips.

Halla ponders what he is mumbling about. Goddess? Pet tigers? He must be delirious, or, it could be the residue of her love potion still playing with his mind. The truth? Does he know her secret, or, is it the incoherent mumblings of someone completely inebriated, she wonders.

As the evening becomes the early hours, Calum rouses from slumber, still reeling from the lingering effects of alcohol. In the stillness of the hotel room, an unexpected sound shatters the tranquillity—a growl, low and blood-curdling, as though a creature from the depths of the night has ventured into his world. Calum's senses heighten, his eyes slowly adjust to the dimness. At the foot of his bed, prowls a mysterious presence. A tiger is in the room, the same one from his dream. Fear clenches at his heart as he strains to discern the shape more clearly in the shadows. Summoning courage, he looks closer. "Oh my god! he gasps, only to discover that the creature is not a tiger. It is Halla.

She is sitting on the floor in a corner of the room at the end of the bed. However, this is not the Halla of the previous night—the confident and self-assured goddess who graced his room. It isn't the volatile girlfriend who challenges his patience. Nor is it the funny, kind, lovable character he had come to know. Instead, a metamorphosis has occurred. She has completely transformed into a vulnerable, troubled version of the witty woman he loves. Knowing her paranoia about dust, he is shocked to see her sitting on the floor, her countenance, a portrait of fear.

"Halla! I thought you went home. What are you doing down there?" concern, etched in his voice. Yet, she remains silent, the weight of her unease, unnerving.

"Come," he implores, extending his hand with care, as though coaxing a delicate creature to his side. She is cold to touch, which is difficult to understand, as the hotel air conditioner is ineffective. He holds her under a blanket warming her while cradling her breasts, one in each hand. In that moment, he senses her fragility, marvelling at the intricate layers that makes up the woman he has come to know and love.

However, by morning, he wakes, to find she is gone.

Chapter Eighteen

Halla is concerned her behaviour from last night at the restaurant may be detrimental to their relationship. With a determination to recultivate his heart and retain the soul of the man who has ignited a spark within her, she decides to refine her approach.

She revels in the intoxicating journey of seduction, where the playground is not only of physical conquest, love potions, but equally, a battlefield of minds. Knowing his predisposition towards the need for compliments, she decides to change the rules of their relationship. Having previously embraced the qualities of female sexuality and elevating it to new heights, the tactic for today is to use another tool of femininity, to lure him back into her realm. "I want," she whispers.

The weakness of men lay nestled within the delicate space of their ego—an insight that women across the globe have known for centuries. With that knowledge and using the magic of her words, the conquest begins, to lionize, flatter and praise. She marvels at the alchemy of using language in a way to transform circumstances. With precision and grace, she calculates a plan to redesign and sculpture their love story in her own unique way.

Halla: I am here. Wait for me in the room, my beautiful kangaroo. I will help you with your luggage.
Calum: Ok, Come on up.

"I am happy you decided to move. Your new place has good air-conditioning. I have looked already before. You will be able to sleep properly. You deserve better," she said, as she tugs at her top, reminding him of the uncomfortable temperature in his room.

Halla has another agenda in mind, the main reason she convinces him to change hotels. She has learned over the years, the best way to live freely is to be a moving target, changing locations, outfits and even personas.

"Yes, I have had enough of this heat now."

"Only one problem," she added.

"What's that?"

"It won't be available to move into until 5pm."

"Oh, why is that?" he asked.

"Between 12 noon and 5pm, it's made available for short term hire. Lovers can rent the room between those hours. The rest of the time, from 5pm until next day, it's for second booking which is what we have...I mean, you have," said Halla, correcting herself.

"Really?" replied Calum. "They rent the room twice in one day. That's clever. For tourists and for lovers on the same day."

"We can leave your luggage in the car and park there. Then we can go walking. I know how you like walking, to stop thinking of me," she added for a response.

He throws her a captivating glance. "Today, I am walking with you. You won't get away without me knowing the truth."

Calum is awe-struck by the sheer scale of the nearby architecture, the Lotte World Tower, a one hundred and twenty-three story sky-scraper located in Sincheon-dong, reaches for the clouds.

"Wow, what a building! It's so huge. This is such a futuristic city," said Calum.

"It is the sixth tallest building in world," she said. "It took thirteen years of planning the site. I was young when this started. Now, look at me."

"You are more beautiful to me every day." Calum turns and holds Halla's face in his hands so she cannot look away.

"There is freedom in acceptance and anguish in resistance," he said.

"Freedom in acceptance. Thank you, my teacher. Can I use that one?" she replied, thinking she didn't ask for a lecture.

"Sure, I just made it up," he laughs.

"I not like heights. I want to show you a beautiful library, if you are brave enough to go on the subway again with me," she teases.

"Are you going to blindfold me again?"

"No, there are no chilies today either. That was before," she joked. Ok, what is the theme for today?"

"Humm, perhaps the opposite."

"What is the opposite of phallus? I cannot begin to imagine," laughed Calum. The air is becoming hot with sexual innuendoes once again.

Calum and Halla catch the subway to a shopping mall, the Coex Mall Starfield Library.

"It looks like a high-rise building made from books. Amazing!" he said, noticing a magnificent display, some 13 meters high. "Everything is so incredibly huge in this city."

"Yes, people donate their books to the library. There is every subject in the world here," said Halla, turning a full 360 degrees, with arms outstretched to emphasise her point.

"Yes, including the Maya no doubt. Amazing!" he commented.

Halla begins her strategy, a plan to conquer him with compliments and praise. "Yes, Mr Discovery Channel. Including the Maya," she said, as they ride an escalator to the next floor.

"Mr. Discovery Channel! Compliments will get you everywhere," replied Calum.

"It's true. I admire you Calum," said Halla. So brave, going to wild places, dangerous places where you don't know people. The jungle. Mosquitoes. Snakes. So brave. My smart kangaroo. My Mr Discovery Channel," as she pulls his arm close to her breast.

"I haven't seen a white snake yet. Lunch?" suggests Calum.

Halla licks her lips. Food is on the menu. "Muuumm, you read my mind," she replied.

"This is very serendipitous that you have brought me here today."

"Seren...dipitous? What is that?" asked Halla.

"Oh, it means fortunate, a nice coincidence," he explained.

"There are no coincidences. Why Calum, is it you think it is seren...dipitous?" replied Halla quizzically.

"I have been planning to give you a copy of my book. I've signed it and there is a special message for you."

Taken back by both the perfect timing and the personal nature of the gift, Halla is transported again into the realm beyond the confines of her immediate surroundings. The signs, the circumstances—they all align in absolute harmony. "It's a perfect collision of time and space," Halla mused, her voice a soft murmur. The boundaries between reality and the enchanting parallel universe they both inhabit, blur once more for her. "The script! It's here with us," she whispers, as she allows herself to marvel at the circumstances that binds them.

"The script! It's here," repeated Halla, her eyes distant and thoughtful.

"The script? What script Halla? That's just my book," Calum said. But for Halla, his gift goes well beyond the 3-dimensional world. Her thoughts are on a galactic scale. She cannot tell him what she knows to be true, not yet.

"Thank you, Calum. This means so much to me," she said, holding Calum's book close to her breast.

The weight of Calum's book in her hands feels more profound than its physical form. The very essence of their connection is encapsulated within its pages. In that moment, she glimpses invisible threads of fate weaving a masterpiece, a story written in the stars, perfectly bound in the pages of their intertwined destinies. There is little doubt in her mind now, that he is the one for her, but he must know her secret. Why isn't he letting on?

"Please read what I wrote to you," said Calum.

"*To my beautiful Mystery Lady…That's me,*" she interjected.

One plus One equals One. We both know our connection is perfect.

I am proud you are with me.

I love you forever.

Calum"

"I am sorry about the small tear in the corner," he said. I have been carrying it in my luggage for a long time, to bring it all the way here, especially for you."

"It's perfect. It has you on it," replied Halla, handling the book like a precious gift. "You are so intelligent. I am amazed."

"Come with me around the world. You can bring your pets," he said, secretly hoping she will consider disposing of the cumbersome animals.

"I want," bowing her head shyly. But then, she notices a sudden change in his body language. It is Calum's turn to become aloof and distant.

"Calum! Where are you?" Halla prods.

"It's what you said. It made me think of the dream I had after you left the other night."

"Oh, what was it I said that reminds you?" she replied.

Calum felt an unease wash over him. Should he tell her about the vision, that it was her who came to his room. Yet, he is curious what the effect would be, if he were to hand her the truth direct.

"I want," he said. "I want, just the same way you said it then. It was in my dream. I am not sure if it was a dream really, more a spiritual experience than a dream. It was just so real, I could touch it," he said, a glazed look in his eyes.

"Oh, I am not sure I should hear the details." replied Halla, preparing herself. Intuitively, she knows it might have a major impact on her, by observation of Calum's intense mood change.

Calum hesitates. "Halla," he whispers, his voice resonates with an air that requires full attention. "I have to say it. It was you. You, were in my dream."

"Me?" replied Halla, her hand resting on her upper chest, protecting her heart.

Calum tries to hold back his honesty, but the words pass his lips. "Yes you. We made...we made love together."

As the weight of his confession settles over her, a cascade of emotions become like the flow of an unstoppable tide. Despite Calum's attempt to deliver the message with as much sensitivity as he can muster, there is no other way to reduce the jolt, than to say it like it is.

"It was beautiful Halla. The most intense experience of my life," he added.

The impact on Halla is profound. It hit her unexpectedly and powerfully, like a white pointer shark attacking a scuba diver in a steel cage. A swirling sea of emotions threatens to consume her. Yet, beneath the surface, there is a realization dawning within her. Her ceremony has worked its mysterious alchemy on Calum. Recovering from the initial shock, she feels a surge of confidence, as if realising she has uncovered the key to an ancient and esoteric magic - a magic that allows her to hold the reins, to command the strongest force in the universe—love.

Halla stands up, her eyes wild and untamed. Then, in a voice, deep and low, as though presiding over a mere mortal. "It's perfect. I know. I am her. She is me." In that second, a glass shatters. A nearby waitress drops her tray on the tiled floor. Halla softens her stance, returning to earth from another dimension. "Excuse me for a moment." She dissipates into the passing crowd.

Calum is stunned by her performance. He has forgotten about his previous suspicions of her leading a double life, a spiritual being one minute, a mortal the next. The memory had lain dormant in his mind, lulled by the exciting moments they have shared as the day progressed. However, his questioning is revived with this sudden outburst. A bewitching paradox resurfaces, becoming the instrument stimulating his detective mind to pursue the truth. But is the truth as elusive as catching a star in his hand? he thought.

How could she have known what transpired in his dream? This enigmatic woman has taken him on a journey of passion and mystery, blurring the lines between reality and fantasy. In his quest for clarity, he is compelled to scrutinize every detail, searching for more clues that will either dispel or confirm his suspicions.

Into the trove of images on his mobile phone he delves, seeking a key that might unlock the secrets of her duality. There, amidst a sea of images he finds the artwork he loves most, which she had sent him early in their relationship. Her painting of a black cat holds a clandestine message. It provokes his scrutiny, captured in a moment of delicate connection with a pink butterfly. They are depicted as though connecting for the first time within her artistic vision. It is too coincidental that they found their way into his dream.

The same dialogue, 'I want', the veiled messages that he would meet a goddess, now this. The evidence is growing in his mind as to her true identity.

Calum steps outside into the warm afternoon air with intention and purpose, guided by an inner compass, directing him toward where Halla may have gone. A determination compels him to confront her directly, yet he is ill-prepared to interrogate the woman who has woven a spell around him. The answers he seeks may not be in her words. He needs to read between the lines.

But now, Halla is running toward him carrying a level of anxiety and fear in her eyes. "Calum, we must hurry! Come with me now," Halla cries, her voice underscored by a sense of urgency.

"What's happened?" Calum questioned, the gravity of the situation causing him alarm.

"We must move fast. Run!" she implored. Calum follows along behind her impatient gait.

A sudden adrenalin rush engulfs him. "Surely, it's not another nuclear missile on the way, is it?"

"No, but it's urgent. Please, hurry!" she insists.

The streets blur as they navigate their way through the bustling city, darting down alleys, through shopping malls and out the other side. Calum's concern deepens with each passing moment. He steals a glance at Halla, her eyes reflecting a mix of anxiety and determination.

"I can walk fast, but running a long distance is out. Tell me what is happening!" his voice, labouring with exhaustion.

"I will soon," Halla assures him, hailing a cab with a well-practiced wave. She looks over her shoulder constantly, her eyes scanning the surroundings for any sign of pursuit. "Quick, get in," she said.

As Calum slid into the backseat of the cab, Halla hands the driver five hundred Korean won. A rapid exchange in her language, hangul ensues. Calum strains to understand, but it is the sudden screech of the taxi tyres that hint at the content of their conversation.

"Halla! I need to know what is going on!" urged Calum.

"There is someone following us again. We need to lose them," she replied, her wild eyes darting toward the shopping centre, disappearing rapidly behind them.

"Again? Who? Who is following us? What do they want?" Calum demands an answer.

"Just give me minute. It's complicated. I need to be sure we have lost them. Then we talk," Halla said, turning to the driver, engaging in another rapid-fire discussion.

"Halla! Are you in some kind of trouble? You need to tell me more than just, its complicated." Calum presses the question, the weight of the unknown bearing down on him, the threat of danger filling the air.

The cab screamed around numerous corners and near misses before Halla is certain her escape strategy is successful. They arrive at Calum's new hotel, the driver having enjoyed the experience, much like a scene from a movie and Calum, sensing Halla has done this before.

"We will be safe here. I don't believe he connects me with you, not yet anyway," her relief becoming evident.

"I am comforted by that. He, who is he? Are you dealing drugs?"

"No, of course not," she protests, the sincerity in her eyes apparent.

The door swings open as they enter the hotel room. "It's much smaller than I remember," comments Halla, still shaking from the experience.

"Then, you remember? Have you been here already?" Calum queried.

"Yes, a long time ago," she replied, her mind drifting back to her youth.

He notices an ashtray near a small window which has an unobstructed view of a massive brick wall approximately two meters away. He lights a cigarette while Halla joins him with a vape. Calum doesn't want to hear about details from her previous life before him, especially concerning a hotel room with a dubious reputation. However, her comment prompts him to clarify something she has said earlier.

"Could it be someone from your past? But you said you haven't been in a relationship for fifteen years?" said Calum, waiting for her to fall into his trap.

"Nice view," she gives him a throw-away line. "Now is not the time to talk about the past!" she snaps.

Brilliant deflection, he thought. "I am waiting, Halla. Who is he? What does this person want with you?"

"I wish it is that simple. I need a drink first," Halla replied, opening the bar fridge door with a sense of purpose. She cracks open a can of beer, blending it with generous amounts of Soju, some of which ends up on the carpet. She hands a glass to Calum, the urgency of their situation eclipsing traditional Korean etiquette.

"Calum, this is hard for me." She takes a long slug of beer. "I told you I am a seer. But there is more to it than that," she said.

"What does being a seer have to do with someone chasing you?"

Halla's phone interrupts their conversation, "Excuse me, one moment," as she retreats to the bathroom. "I am sorry. I have to take this."

Calum is alone processing the disruption to their day. "Never a dull moment," he murmurs to himself with his ear to the bathroom overhearing Halla's hushed conversation, not understanding a word. The tone sounds hostile, raising more questions about the unusual situation. Halla returns, not before Calum retains his original position. She retrieves another beer from the fridge.

"Halla, I love you. You can tell me anything," Calum reassured, a pledge to stand by her side regardless of the revelation. "Drugs, prostitution, an ex-husband, whatever the outcome," he promises, he will stay her friend.

"He is from another world," Halla throws the answer to Calum like a hand grenade, his visibly shocked expression reflects the absurd events taking place. "He is from a movie I watched," she added.

"Oh, an actor," said Calum, somewhat relieved.

"No...well, sort of... He is a character in a movie," she continues.

"I see. I am pleased you are only feeding me small bits of credibility at a time," said Calum, adding sarcasm, an attempt to revive a sense of normality to the conversation.

Halla has started her explanation and is now compelled to continue. "You see, I am a portal where actors come into this world to continue their drama. They often don't want their part in a movie to end, so they try and find a way to cross over. I am that bridge through which they come. Do you understand me?"

"Sure. Let's have another drink. I don't have a problem with any of this. It's not something out of the unusual," he replied, realising he is trivialising her explanation.

"Oh Calum. I am so alone with this. They no understand me. You are the first one I've told. Now you are part of my life, it's only a matter of time before you would know this...that I am different," she confides.

Calum persists for more information. "So, what you are telling me, they are from the next world? They don't understand? Who are they?"

"They?....No, this world. They are the creation of writers, so in a sense, from here. It's hard to explain. My English, not so good," she said, with a hint of regret.

"Then, which movie is this man from?" asks Calum, suspecting he is not only in a foreign country, but also with someone who is from another planet.

"It's the man from Raiders of the Lost Ark."

"Harrison Ford! Well, who else would it be?" replied Calum, suspecting the woman he loved might have serious mental problems.

"No, it's the one who he shot in the market. He was only on screen for a few minutes or so. Have you seen the film?" she inquires.

"A long time ago...I cannot remember who you mean. I would have to see the movie again," said Calum, mentally going through the scenes he could recall. "I just remember a big ball rolling down the hill after Indiana Jones."

"I knew it would be difficult for you, a mortal, to understand. You probably think I have mental health issues."

"I am not qualified to be the judge of that," Calum said. "Have you had other actors trying to get into the world? What do you mean by, mortal?"

But the answer to this question lay too close to their relationship for her to reply.

"I am afraid of him," she said, hugging herself as though providing a protective shield, emphasising the loneliness of her journey.

Calum is looking at his hands. "This is strange. I don't recognise my hands. he said in amazement.

"Your hands? What do you mean?"

"They look totally different. I must be overtired."

Beads of sweat forms on Halla's forehead. It is time for her to escape Calum's sight. "Can I use the shower please?" Halla asks, while moving toward the bathroom. But she has a final retreating comment before she leaves in the hope of adding weight to her credibility. "Calum, you are a writer. You dream people from your imagination. They become real. The characters become part of our consciousness. I know you will come to understand over time."

Only a short time has elapsed until she re-enters the bedroom however, Calum has nodded off, the stress of the day exhausting him. Now Halla has an opportunity to look upon the man who has entered her life and changed it forever. She moves closer to him, but not before shedding her towel. Holding his hands in hers and examining them closely, she whispers softly, "It's happening my love. He is you. You are him."

As though re-enacting a well-rehearsed event, she reaches for the tv remote, flicking through the numerous channels, stopping on number 260. It is the 'adults only' selection showing short extracts of pornographic video clips.

Waking from a semi-conscious state, Calum can hear the low-level TV audio sounds of Asian women making unrestrained pleasurable moans. He becomes conscious she is setting the mood with the lights turned low, her nude body pressing against him, an indicator of what might be on the agenda. He responds by putting his arm around her.

She begins to feel like a precious pearl encased within the strength of the shell of a clam. "I am so afraid," she whispers. "But when I am with you, I feel safe and protected." Calum pulls her closer, feeling the warmth of her body against his.

Her hand slips down low beneath the sheets and brushes his erect phallus. "Oh, I found a chilli," she giggles, whereupon, she unravels it from beneath the bedding.

She marvels at her capacity to bring his penis to life, for it is the magic of her femineity that compels it to respond as it does.

Her other hand, is between his legs, tickling his testicles playfully, revelling in the effect it has on him. Calum has the urge to raise his hips and push upward. She enjoys the feeling of a hot throbbing penis between her fingers. The intensity of love and lust building, their heart rate increases and their breathing becomes pronounced. Halla responds by parting her legs wider. It's been a long time since she held a man like this.

"Can I kiss? I find a gochu. I am hungry?" she said, prodding his raised phallus.

What man could resist such a question? he thought. The request virtually went without requiring an answer, but he is quick to add an element of humour.

"Hummm, let me think about that for a while." Then he added without hesitation. "Ok, you can."

Halla responds enthusiastically. "But no photos." Her tongue lashes the full length of his now rock-hard manhood. "Nice chilli," she teases, accompanied by her signature purring vocal effects. "A monster," her bright shiny eyes, reflects the increased moisture forming between her thighs. "It's as hard as the sculpture you kissed," she laughs.

"Stay with me again tonight," he pleads, but an answer never came. "Our time is small," he continued, wondering if the dream he had a few nights previously, is about to be revisited in reality. He is now excited about a sequel.

"Can I keep you," he murmurs, hoping to hear the now familiar response. "I want, she replied, knowing that is the answer he likes to hear.

Halla is swept up in sharing the ecstasy of an intimate moment. She has dreamed of spending time like this with the one she loves and now, it is a reality.

"I have a hungry lion with me," said Calum.

That comment proves to be bad timing. During their union, an unstoppable emotional surge of fragility, anger and loss swells from within Halla's heart.

She remembers the experience of her mother. It reminds her, that what she holds in her hand, is often used as a weapon of warfare, a means to humiliate, denigrate and degrade women. Now, it is in the flesh, in tangible form within her grasp. Images of the brutality of the Japanese impact on her gender and family races through her mind and it is this, a male throbbing muscle, that is the cause of so much suffering. Control of her mind is increasingly impossible. Other thoughts come to her of circumstances, reminding her of her childless life, now an impossible dream. The window of opportunity is virtually closed permanently for her to fulfil the biological urge to reproduce. Her time is small. The words repeat endlessly. Our time is small. I want. Calum will soon be leaving, perhaps, never to see him again. They envelop her mind, gnawing at her, clawing and scratching at her soul. Our time is small. I want. Our time is small. I want.

"Ouw!" Calum cries, as he pulls himself away from her sudden, excessively hard clenched teeth. "Why did you do that?"

Like the rapid melt of an ice cream in a microwave, his penis retreats to safety, away from the possibility of more savagery bearing down upon its defenceless form.

"That's enough for you fella," a statement made lacking in tenderness, like she had just thrown out some useless garbage.

"Fella?" replied Calum, surprised she even knew the word.

"You not come back. You leave me alone. I want. I want. Blar! Blar! Blar!" Her tone cut the air as sharp as knives as she stalks the room from corner to corner. "You have women in every country. I am nothing. Spilt milk!"

"That's not true. Halla. It's you I want. Stop that," he said, trying to recover the bliss of the now terminated intimate moment. However, there is no soothing balm forthcoming to ease the discomfort for both his mind or his private parts.

"I know. I know," she retaliates, a light slap to his face. "I know you leave me alone! Mystery lady! Mystery ladies everywhere. Blah! Blah! Blah!" she said, as she pulls her clothes on impatiently. Knocking the top off another bottle of soju, she slams down the contents hurriedly, accentuating the palpable tension in the air. In the background, the audio sounds of pleasure and ecstasy send contrasting signals to a room full of emotional conflict and hostility.

Calum endeavours to convince her to return to his embrace. "Stop Halla! You have had enough to drink."

"Not need man. Not need man. You want.. I want ...You want your fantasy dream. Mr Discovery!" as she points to the tv screen. "I no good enough. I want. I want!" comes the verbal eruption from within her deep-rooted insecurities.

"Please stop!" pleads Calum. "You are jealous, but you are jealous of yourself. It was you who came to me in the dream."

But it is all going wrong for Halla. Beads of sweat are forming again across her forehead, adding physical discomfort to her already disturbed mental state.

"Hungry lion. Fuck off! Go and diversify the species with a..female kangaroo!" The door slams and she is outside in the hallway. "Mortals!" screams Halla, not caring who hears her.

Calum is perplexed and confused, a state of mind to which he is becoming accustomed. "Mortals?" he repeated. "What the?" Yet this time, he promises himself not to chase an inconsolable drunk woman, instead, he turns up the volume of channel 260. Clenched teeth and verbal abuse, are not his favourite aphrodisiac. "Do I need to see her again?" he questions. However, deep within the corridors of his mind, he knows that to become the best version of himself, means to accept her in all her complexities, unconditionally.

Calum is mostly unaware of the complex weight of social influences bearing down on Halla from her culture and from her past. However, he acknowledges that the suffering inflicted on Korean women by the Japanese is largely because of one thing, the demands of men's primal urge which Halla had just held in her hands. But he questions why he has to suffer, innocent of any wrongdoing.

Chapter Nineteen

Mongee is not sure if she knows the person who enters the unit, choosing to retreat and cringe under the bed upon Halla's return. She is joined by Songee. Their owner has a different energy about her as she carries her heavy mood into their peaceful environment. Halla's anger held back her tears for when she was outside in public, but now, away from prying eyes and in the safety of her home, a heartfelt torrent of emotion and regret is unleashed. Reaching for her phone, her fingers shake with fearful remorse.

Halla: I am so sorry. I don't know what is wrong with me. Will you ever forgive me?

A return text never came back to her. Calum is intent on his television program, the volume exceeding the level of the text signal.

Halla: Please reply. Please tell me you forgive me.

Halla explores the contents of her fridge. As usual, there is very little in there that is edible, save for a bottle of soju, three cans of beer and a small bowl of rice. She rips the top off a can, hoping it will be enough to escape the grip of her confused mind. However, she is starting to lose herself.

With a sigh, she grasps another can, tearing at the entrance in a desperate attempt to silence the conflict within. This additional beer is still insufficient to liberate her from the clutches of her mind. The essence of who she once was, slipping through her fingers, now, she is mercurial and lost. Instability grips Halla, the ground beneath her feet crumble away piece by piece. Her identity slips through the cracks, leaving behind a woman entangled in the threads of an alternate reality. "The woman I once was!" she spat, her words laced with frustration and defiance. The boundaries blur, as Halla teeters on the edge of a surreal precipice, desperately clinging to the fragments of her vanishing self.

To her sacred space she returns where, 'Jacheongbi', the Goddess of love presides. The seeds from the Ginkgo tree she has collected are laid out on her mother's table. Turning the worn pages of the ancient compendium, she pauses on a page, 'Transfiguration of the Soul'. In subtext is written. 'Use with extreme caution'.

Halla lights three candles, arranged in a triangle, the same configuration as the last time she performed her love ceremony, only this time, the candles are black. The two dolls representing the bond between her and Calum are in the centre, bound in marijuana leaves, cat fur covering their modesty.

From the plant that predates history, she meticulously crushes the Ginkgo berries into a velvety paste, resolute not to let the potent fragrance sway her determination. To this, is adds crushed dinosaur bone, sourced from Mongolia and a tiny amount of fine powder, comprised of meteorite dust. She believes her conjuration challenges the universe, fracturing the very fabric of time itself.

As if participating in an ancient tribal ceremony, she paints her face with the Gingko paste concoction. Her sense of self gradually resurfacing, as she draws a zigzag pattern across her forehead. On her cheeks, another series of lines draw attention to the centre between her eyes, her third eye. With a graceful artful stroke, she follows the contours of her chin, journeying along her jawline towards each ear, completing the mystical canvas of her countenance. Her reflection in the mirror appeals.

"This is me," she smiles, satisfied at what she believes is her authentic self.

The same ingredients she tricked Calum into taking previously, Horney Goat weed, Sichuan peppercorn and halogenic mushrooms, are now mingled together. To this, she adds blended Brazil nuts which she believes reconnects DNA strands, and a thimble of ayahuasca from deep within the jungles of the Amazon. Leaving no room for error, she concludes the recipe of transfiguration with Ambergris, from the gut of sperm whales. All these magical elements are seamlessly blended in a vessel of magic, ready to weave its spell upon whoever receives its potent contents.

She smears moisture from her vagina over the dolls. Then she wraps a snake made of white clay around them as they face each other in an intimate embrace. Upon lighting the cat fur, they smoulder together. A small plume of smoke rises, which she inhales. She coughs, then her chant begins.

"Warm seed, love run strong; warm heart, let us never part."

Halla opens the stain-glass window where she sees the lights of the Olympic bridge, reminding her of her purpose; to help her lover understand the intimate connection they share between this realm and the next. Mongee and Songee huddle anxiously together under a couch.

The reception phone rings in Calum's room. But first, channel 260 needs to be switched off.

"Yes, Calum here," he answers, shifting attention away from the video programs with some difficulty.

"There is someone here in foyer…see you. They know name you," said the receptionist in broken English.

"Me? Ok, tell them I will meet them in ten minutes. Thank you," Calum said, as he puts the phone down. Who could it be? He can only recognise two people in Korea who might know his name. It could be Mr 7.30, seeking an explanation of why he left his accommodation, or perhaps Halla, returning to apologise. ''Why doesn't she just text me?" Calum wonders.

As he enters the foyer, he is looking for Halla however, it is a tall bearded man who greets him. He is dressed in loose fitting black clothes accentuated by a red belt tied at his waist. Calum is shocked as the man heads straight to him, as though the strange visitor has prior knowledge of what Calum looks like.

"Calum Wilkins? Pleased to meet you," he said, extending his hand. "Sit down, please. We need to talk…about my niece, Halla," he added, in an official, determined tone.

"Your niece?" said Calum, unable to disguise his surprise at the new information and even more unbelievable, the man has a middle eastern appearance.

"Yes, I… we, the family, want to know how she is and where she is," the man continued.

"I don't know. She left earlier." replied Calum, feeling more than a little suspicious. "I don't know where she lives. She won't give me her address."

The man senses Calum's disbelief. "Don't concern yourself with my appearance. I married into the family." He leans forward to emphasise a point. "You see, we want to convince her to go back," he said.

"Go Back? Back where?" Calum asked.

"To the ward, Mr Wilkins," the man finishes his sentence. "You see, Halla is a psychiatric patient here in Seoul."

Halla: Calum, please call. I am worried. I love you.

"Psychiatric patient! Oh no," said Calum, reeling from the tsunami of incoming verbal shock waves.

"Yes, she is. You see, we cannot make her go back to the ward unless there is evidence of self-harm. It's against the law, but we can convince her to make the right choice, for her own good. It's her mental health and well-being that concerns us," pressing the point with concern in his voice.

Calum is being swayed by the man's emotional state. "So, what do you want me to do? Where do I fit in?"

"I...we, understand you have a connection with her. If you could call me when you see her next. Here is my number," he said, handing Calum a card.

"Ok, I was starting to wonder if she is alright, mentally, I mean. I haven't got her address. She won't give it to me," he reiterated.

"You are right to question her sanity. But I am curious. What exactly is your relationship with her?"

"Friends, just friends, nothing more." said Calum. The last thing he wanted, is to be seen taking advantage of a woman suffering with severe mental health problems.

"Thank you, Mr Wilkins, for your support. It's so sad, that I now have such a small part to play in her life. We used to be so close," the man confided.

Calum notices his comment being oddly familiar. *'A small part to play.'* Is this the person Halla is trying to escape from, the movie character, who has entered the physical world? But he scolds himself for allowing Halla's fantastical stories to influence him.

"Oh, I am sorry to hear that. If I see her again, I will call you," Calum commiserated.

"Thank you," the man replied, as he got up to leave. "Her mother is beside herself with worry."

"Her mother? Halla told me she had passed," replied Calum.

"Halla lives in a fictitious world of make believe, Mr Wilkins. Alcohol and a host of other things, sometimes all at the same time. There will be repercussions if we don't get to her soon."

"I am not sure I can help?" said Calum, uncertain if the comment about repercussions, is a veiled personal threat.

"She is delusional, Mr Wilkins. She thinks she is a goddess one day, then a star from her favourite movie, the next. It goes on. I cannot talk about this anymore. It's so upsetting. Thank you for your time," said the man, visibly disturbed, as he exits the foyer.

"I will do what I can," Calum shouted after him, as he returns to his room. The meeting left him perplexed, sensing it was more an interrogation, than a call for assistance.

The door closes behind him leaving him alone with the weight of conflicting emotions, torn between duty and desire. He is committed to the woman he loves, a force that binds him to her with a passionate devotion. Yet, now the spectre of uncertainty looms. Should his allegiance be solely to her family, who hold the secrets of her past, the intimate details that shape the woman he cares for. The dilemma pulls him in conflicting directions. His responsibility as a protector and an honour-bound companion urges him to reach out to her family, to seek their guidance and assistance. They, after all, are the custodians of her well-being. However, in making such a decision, he risks being perceived as a traitor by Halla, the woman with who he shares a secret bond.

On the other hand, the ramifications of inaction bear down on him. If he chooses to remain silent, to withhold the truths that he suspects lay hidden in the shadows, he faces the grave consequence of imperilling Halla's life, a journey of alcohol and drug addiction, from which there may be no escape.

Love, duty, and loyalty, each step is laden with the gravity of disastrous outcomes. He longs to protect the woman who has captured his heart, to shield her from conflict. Yet, the path ahead is obscured by uncertainty, and Calum knows that whatever choice he makes will shape both their destinies.

Halla: Calum, I feel something terrible has happened.
Calum: Don't worry, Everything will be ok in the end.
Halla: They have got to you, haven't they! I know.

"They, who are they? he wonders. How can she possibly know someone has contacted him.

Within the confines of Calum's mind, reality is becoming an elusive paradigm, pirouetting on the precipice of truth and deception. In this ethereal expanse, he wrestles with the notion that the boundaries between what is real and what's mere illusion is blurring into uncertainty. It is Halla who has set him on this newfound perspective. Life for him has evolved into a grand masquerade, a cosmic stage, where every soul plays a part, donning masks of joy, sorrow, love, and despair. The lines between authenticity and artifice, become indistinct on his horizon of comprehension. As Calum navigates the intricate choreography of existence, he finds some solace in the concept that, perhaps, the beauty of life lays in the perpetual void between reality and illusion.

Calum: Where are you?
Calum: Come back. I am leaving Korea soon.

Several minutes later a reply comes.

Halla: I am outside your door. Let me in please.

Calum opens the door. Halla's hands are full, while awkwardly removing her shoes.

"Allow me," said Calum, as he assists with some of her load. She reeks of alcohol but looked intoxicatingly beautiful in a sleek black dress, white pearls framing her femininity.

"You look irresistible," complimented Calum, totally forgetting his previous concerns, her beauty distracting him momentarily from rational thought. "Your face! You look incredible."

Not letting compliments sway her from her mission, Halla spoke. "Well Calum, Tell me. Are you with me, or with him? "Do you believe me or do you have suspicions now?" she said, convinced the verdict has already been reached. "Before you answer, I want you to take a look at this," she added. Halla retrieves her mobile phone. It is cued on a YouTube video showing a scene from the Hollywood movie, Raiders of the Lost Ark.

"What are you showing me Halla?" quizzed Calum.

"Watch this and tell me if you recognise anyone." She releases the play button.

The scene depicts a busy marketplace where Indiana Jones is searching for Marian Raven. After a series of fights and Prat falls, the crowd separates to reveal a man who is challenging Indiana Jones in a duel. He is waving a massive sword about in a threatening manner. Indiana chooses to shoot him, as opposed to engaging in a fight. "Does this man look familiar?" says Halla, as she presses the pause button, showing a man dressed in black, a red belt at his waist.

Calum needs time to absorb the revelation. The actor in the scene is identical to the man who he met at his hotel. At first, he is speechless, then he finds the words.

"Halla, that's him. That's the man who met with me in the foyer today. I am so sorry I doubted you. This is beyond my comprehension," he said, as his world-view comes crashing down.

"I forgive you Calum." Halla pulls him closer. "I know it's hard to believe. As you can see, he is only on the screen for a few seconds. He wanted more and argued with the director about not having any dialogue."

Calum pressed her for an answer. "But what does he want with you?"

"He believes that because he came through me into reality, I can help him. I can't. He has to find his own way home," she explained.

"Like all of us. No one can do it for us," Calum expanded upon her comment. "We have to do it ourselves. I understand that," he added. "Which reminds me, he didn't give me his name," said Calum, as he retrieved the man's card. "369, that is supposed to be a telephone number? Just a number. No name."

"He doesn't have one. He doesn't have a name in the film either," said Halla. "Yet somehow, he trick his way into my family."

Calum doesn't understand the meaning of the number, yet Halla knows it is a secret message meant especially for her.

"Nameless. Homeless. Restless. Searching...forever searching," she continued.

"Sounds like most of the people on the planet." Calum continued, with a tinge of remorse considering his own life. "This is too spooky," he added.

"Yes, searching, like you and me. For our way home," said Halla. "To love. He is searching...and found you, which means, he is not far from me."

"But we found each other. That is the main thing," said Calum. "This is totally outside of my experience. And to think I have come into contact with one of these…I don't even know what they are called."

"Walk Ins. But it doesn't end there." Halla held back from continuing, mentally debating if she should give him more information now, or wait. She is uncertain if he will understand the special dynamics that has been building around their relationship since the first day they met. She chooses to keep the mysterious qualities of their love affair, that she knows to be true, to herself, for now.

"You were saying? It doesn't end there. What doesn't end there?" said Calum, annoyed she doesn't finish the sentence.

"Come, I have a celebratory drink I have prepared for us to share," she said, as she removes two glasses from her bag, placing one in his hand. "It's our last night together before you leave me alone," a regretful tone to her voice.

"What's this? Another nightcap?" quizzed Calum, an innocent bystander in the events about to unfold.

"It will help us both relax," she said.

In Korean style, she ceremoniously pours them both a drink.

"Remember, she said. "One hand on the inside of arm or on your heart, like this."

"I remember," said Calum. "I always will and I will always remember you," he added. "To be in love for just one day is more valuable, than ten years of heartache or separation."

"Yes, just one day in love, more valuable," she repeats.

Halla lit three candles bringing a romantic ambience to the room. Raising her glass high, she said, "Geon bae, my Mr Discovery," to which Calum replied, "Geon bae, my fire in the sky."

They both drank the contents. Halla knows it will be only a matter of time before the magic starts working on them.

Calum sweeps his hand near her breast, as she removes her exquisite black dress. "Halla, I can feel a heat coming from within your breast. It feels like you are overheating. Unbelievable! Radiating fire!"

"I will be a fire in the sky for you," she promises. She holds these words to have an eternal truth, believing their destinies are bound together by a promise, a collaboration with the complexity of the universe.

"My fire in the sky," Calum repeated.

"It's our last night together before you are taken from me," said Halla, sorrow echoing through her voice.

"I am here with you until the sunrise, and you know I will be back," he replied. They kiss for the first time, then they drink the potion.

"Our first kiss," said Calum.

"Does it still hurt," said Halla, pointing towards Calum's genital area. "I am so sorry," she added.

"No, I am good." he smiled.

"Lay back and relax my love. We are together now. That is all that matters," said Halla. "Warm seed, love run strong; warm heart, let us never part," she added, which Calum repeats.

"I want" said Calum, as though his promise is binding for all time.

"Feel, don't think," she whispers. "We will find our way home. Love will be our guiding light. Salanghaeyo."

All is calm with their intimate moment. But then, everything changes, again.

The rapid flickering of the bedside lamp begins, as the ceiling fan reverses direction. Snowflakes return to the ice-cold room which transforms into stardust. The low sound of Buddhist prayer bowls begin. The atmosphere pulses with an otherworldly energy in readiness for the arrival of another super-natural event.

As a violent earthquake shakes the foundations, Calum and Halla are confronted, yet steadfast. They lay on a bed transformed. It consists of numerous white snakes which curl beneath them, over their nudity and between. In the midst of the ethereal transfiguration, the once ordinary room becomes an enchanted domain of love and lust. The wall paint blisters and liquifies as the walls themselves, buckle and bend with intensity. The candles, casting fleeting shadows are in tandem with the lovers' metamorphosis and union. The ceiling fan hovers in space, mirroring the change in the structure of time, above which is a vast blackness. With the union of their physical bodies, initiated by a redeeming kiss of forgiveness, they join.

Calum and Halla, entwined on the bed, experience a profound transmutation on a soul level, as a torrent of sinuous forms curl beneath and over the nakedness of the lovers. It is a union not only of physical bodies but also of realms—the Korean Goddess and now, the initiated, transformed Calum.

In his grasp, a majestic staff emerges, crowned by the regal head of a raven. In the bird's beak, cradles a vibrant crystal, suspended, floating above a mesmerizing pool of mercury. The crystal pulses with mystical energy, and then, with Herculean strength, Calum drives the staff into the Earth's mantle. In that instant, Halla, overcome with ecstasy, releases a melodic cry that echoes across the terrestrial landscape of the entire surface of the earth.

The atmosphere responds in kind, as oceans roar and winds howl on this stormy night. Thunderous clouds gather, and lightning illuminates the celestial stage. In the midst of this cosmic tournament, Calum holds his mysterious Korean Queen in his arms, their love forged in the primal cadence of the elements.

Beneath them, blew a threatening cloud of volcanic ash from which the roar of lions reverberate-a savage manifestation of power and primal energy, all that is dark and separate. A horde of these screeching creatures, their intent nefarious, scratch and claw, adding foreboding danger to their celestial journey. As they navigate the tumultuous terrain, the lovers find solace in each other's arms. Mounted on a powerful white stallion, they gallop across a landscape of burning sulphur—treacherous and rugged, a metaphor for the challenges they once faced, but now victorious at last, they escape to freedom and eternal bliss.

The journey leads them to the embrace of soft white clouds, where the sanctity of their love is cradled in the arms of the universe. In this cosmic cocoon, they transform into embryonic seeds within the womb of creation, twins, poised to embark on a new cycle of existence, not alone, but conjoined as one.

Across the universe a profound silence envelopes Calum with his Queen by his side. Only the primal sound, the heartbeat of the cosmos, echoes in the vast, resplendent expanse. In that hushed stillness, they became synchronised with the cosmic symphony, their love a glorious eternal flame in the grand design of existence.

They return, to say goodbye, the sheets wet from physical exertion and the melt of drifting snow.

Chapter Twenty

The bittersweet ache of the farewell, a haunting memory imprinted forever on their souls, an indelible moment, as time, the merciless sculptor of destinies, moves on.

Halla is left standing alone, her world fades away leaving only the silhouette of Calum's hand in her memory, pressed against the cold glass window of the departing bus.

Incheon international airport looms large as the bus comes to a halt. This is the place only three weeks earlier, where Calum had arrived on a flight from Thailand. A transformation has swept over his life. Now, he feels different, a person he can hardly recognise, both mentally and physically. The landscape of his heart has shifted, unveiling a version of himself that is unfamiliar, yet exhilarating. Someone is on his mind now who wasn't there before when he first arrived in this mysterious land. He has acquired additional luggage, a lady who he wonders if she is either a fallen Korean goddess or a powerful conjuror. He questions if he will ever know the truth. Regardless, she is a weight he is only too willing to carry, as love has lightened the load. Like an unexpected gift, she is becoming an integral part of his journey, a passenger in the expedition of his heart. Alone again, he is about to board another flight, this time to the Americas.

Who was I passed this way?

Who now, passes here?

The answer hangs suspended.

According to the flight booking officer at Korean Air, Calum had forgotten one important detail, "I cannot let you on the flight," she said.

"What! Why not?" He protested.

"You don't have an updated e-visa for the USA," said the flight attendant. "It is out of date," she added.

"But I am only transiting. Not stopping in the USA."

"That is the aviation rules. We have to abide by."

Halla: Please call me when you get to the airport. I love you, my kangaroo.

Calum is devastated. He has only three hours to get a visa or, it would mean staying in Korea, therefore missing his flight. This is something he can't afford.

"I cannot believe I overlooked this detail," Calum cursed. He quickly fills out the on-line application form and is about to press send, when his mobile phone battery loses power.

"Bat-er-ly! Bat-er-ly Bat-er-ly! he repeats Halla's reaction in the restaurant days earlier. Stressed and agitated, he searches for the location of a charging station. Then, it's the frustration of having to wait for his phone to have enough power to finish the process. Minutes seem like hours.

Halla: Why you leave so early to airport?

She doesn't understand the need to get to departures early, not having done international travel before. Calum likes to be ahead of time as a precaution, if something like this type of problem is to eventuate. "Sounds like she is angry again," he said to himself.

He decides not to reply to that text immediately. There are more important things to get done. "There, it's away! Now it's a waiting game." he sighs. Is he able to compress seventy-two hours, the suggested application timeframe, into two and a half? It looks like he might be in Seoul again tonight. As much as he wants to be with Halla out of concern for her safety, it is too late to change his itinerary.

Calum: I have arrived at airport. I miss you. Bo go si pur yo.

Calum is under surveillance again, by the man who had met with him at his hotel foyer. Surprised Halla is nowhere to be seen, he has mistakenly thought they would both be making an escape overseas together.

After a hurried dash through customs, the aircraft leaves the tarmac, with it, all physical connection with Korea. The seat beside him remains unoccupied, a poignant reminder of the void left by her absence. As the city lights disappear under the wing of the aircraft, the only consolation is that he would see her again in a few months. I suppose she is at home with her pets, recovering from the late nights they had spent together, he pondered. Exhausted, it isn't long before he is fast asleep. Then, the plane suddenly touches down in Seattle, America, 11 hours later. It seemed like a 30-minute flight to him. A quick transfer and then it is on to Canada for a reunion with his daughter.

Calum: I made it to America. I love you and miss you a lot and I don't like you.

"What is he doing in America?" Halla whispered, her suspicious mind activated. "He said he is going to be in Canada. Probably meeting some girl, or his ex. I hate him."

Halla: You must be exhausted. I don't like you either. I miss you.
Halla: Calum! Thank you for always supporting and trusting me. I think I met a reliable kangaroo.
Calum: I wish you were here with me safely in Canada. I know you have responsibilities.
Halla: I had a hard time following the kangaroo. I hope to be with you one day.
Calum: Whatever was in that drink, I want some more. I had another dream last night. About me and you.
Halla: Me too. You were in mine.
Calum: You will always be in my dreams. But I want you for real. I feel changed.
Calum: I want to call you and talk about it.
Halla: If we talk about, we weaken the experience. There no words to describe.
Halla: You said it. Feel, don't think.
Calum: Yes, I said that. Feel don't think. Remember the feeling.

"He is gone," whispers Halla. It is like the aftermath of a cyclone that has passed over her. Halla's previous life returns, now with the weight of solitude. She had this feeling when he went to Busan, but its far more intense, the stillness suffocating, wrapping her in a shroud of despondency. The inertia of the atmosphere, eventually taking its toll. The lure of sleep invites her to escape where she finds refuge from the confrontation of harsh reality. Mongee is relieved to have the company of her master again, offering silent reassurance that Halla is not alone on her journey. They find solace in each other's company.

Calum: I have made it to my daughter's place safely. Very tired.

Calum worries what is going through her mind. This is a test of their relationship. Will she appreciate returning to her previous life without him? She might feel relieved. The comfort of familiarity and predictability, versus the readjustment of having the demands of a partner to consider. He knows he isn't easy to be around for an extended period. Even more so, for someone with English as a second language.

Halla: Get some rest. It was a long flight.

Calum has the responsibility of house-sitting for his daughter which includes caring for her kitten while she works away. It is a perfect opportunity to reconnect with her in Canada and to be grounded for a while. He has been travelling for almost a year. Having a base is a welcome relief from organising hotel accommodation, exchange rates and flights.

Calum: I am not happy leaving you alone without me being there to help you. I am worried about that strange man.
Halla: It's ok. I will deal with it. It's not the first time.
Calum: It's a constant worry for me. Wish you were here safe with me.
Halla: Me too.
Calum: I have something I would like to share with you.
Calum: It's an observation...just something I have noticed in life. I could email it to you if you have time to read. It's not that long. I call it a 'Knock on the door.
Halla: Yes, send it to me. I miss you.
Calum: Ok, here it goes. I will email it. I hope you understand my English.
Halla: Yes. I can read English better than speaking.

Life, an Invitation to Attend.

(A knock on the door)

Let's suppose it is true that we have guardian angels.

Their purpose is to help us live life to the fullest possible extent and experience. To be free and to live without fear. That's their job because to be free of fear, is the gate way to the heavenly realm toward true joy and happiness.

Let's just suppose that is true.

So, when we least expect it, they knock on our door. The guardian angels send down to earth an *Invitation to attend life*. It may take the form of a person, an encounter, a creative idea (we think is our own) perhaps a challenge that will expand our understanding and experience. Invariably, it involves us moving out of our comfort zone.

We have a choice. Will we go with the invitation or, postpone the opportunity.

If we say yes, I will, then wonderful things happen. Fear, although present, is not standing in the way. More importantly, the angels will send more invitations, one after another. Life becomes buoyant and full.

If we choose 'no', then things pretty well stay the same. An individual loses the opportunity to expand their consciousness and level of awareness. Life becomes grey and somehow repetitive, looking more like death in motion.

We ponder the *'invitation to attend'* and decide, will I take the risk or hold back. Holding back is counter-productive to living life without fear.

I have received numerous 'invitations to attend' which I have learned to accept and they keep coming.

I invited you for a coffee. You accepted my invitation and Halla, look at us now! So glad you did!

Essentially what I am saying is the colours of the rainbow of life are made more vivid when we recognise these invitations, accept the challenge without fear and undertake the journey as a means to enhance this beautiful experience called life.

It's just something I believe might be true that I wanted to share. Thanks for reading.

Halla: Lots in this to think about.
Halla: Perhaps, I invited you.
Calum: And I accepted your invitation.

Halla lays on the bed stroking her cat, her fingers gently tracing the patterns in her fur. "Maybe it's time I told him," she confides. "Now he is gone, it's safe. He is out of the country. I've held back for so long." Songee rolls over indicating her other side needs attention.

Halla: I have something to share with you too. Something challenging.

She searches through her favourite DVD movie collection. They are meticulously catalogued according to genre, an organised arrangement that mirrors the order she seeks in her own life. Under the heading of romance, one in particular stands out, marked with three stars. A decision weighs on her, a mental contest between hesitation and wanting. She holds it close to her breast, hoping for a relief that has plagued her for weeks. Halla sends Calum a link to a movie, The Bridges of Madison County.

"There, it is away," she whispers. It has been on her mind from the moment she first met Calum, which seems like an eternity ago. She hopes this will be the conduit for the unspoken words held captive for so long, a secret finally set free. Her mind is laden with a mix of uncertainty and anticipation.

Halla: I really want you to see this movie. It's my favourite romance. I send you a link.
Calum: Sure, I will watch it. The Bridges of Madison County. I haven't seen it before.
Halla: I have seen it about 10 times.
Halla: After I met a kangaroo, I remember this movie right away. I don't have husband but I haven't been in love for a long time, and you're a free traveller around the world.

Calum isn't sure why she is intent on him watching this movie. Being a romance, perhaps it might have some bearing on their relationship, he thought. If so, he needs some clarification before seeing it, so that during the movie, he might understand her better.

Calum: Halla, do you see yourself in the movie?
Halla: Is it possible for people with different environments and values to be together...a question of.
Halla: I felt a lot of things from this movie before I met you. It's a good movie in many ways. Let's talk after you watch it.
Calum: My Halla is a romantic at heart...it's contagious...I look forward to watching it. I love you a lot.
Halla: I see so many similarities. Good night.
Calum: Ok, I will call tomorrow.

Calum is in a fortunate position with access to a wide-screen television. With the first snow falling outside and a fireplace burning bright, he sits back with his daughter's kitten, Molly, prepared for anything. "Winter is here at last," he sighs. "At last."

He rarely watches romantic movies, preferring science fiction. The opening scenes of the movie begin. "Some similarities?" commented Calum.

Even with jet-lag affecting him, he is unable to pull himself away from the screen. As the storyline unfolds, Calum finds himself both captivated and disturbed. Coincidences evolve which seem to intertwine both their lives with that of the characters. He is amazed. For anyone with a logical, practical mind, there is undeniable evidence of the uncanny parallels between the movie and their story, he thought. It's what Halla observed from the beginning, since they first met and avoided telling him.

Calum: This movie is about us, you know. It is a sad movie. I don't want you in a sad movie with me...We should do a happy one.

Upon reading Calum's comment, Halla felt at last her view of reality is justified. The anxiety over the last few weeks weighed heavy, just as confronting as watching Calum's bus disappear down the highway to the airport. Now, there is a sense of relief. He could see it too. She isn't imagining the connection. She celebrated by filling a glass with soju, believing his response is the result of her love potion triggering a deeper awareness of their connection. "Geon bae!" she said.

Halla: Do you think so too. I kept thinking about the movie during our time. They gave up their love for responsibility.

The events over the previous three weeks were becoming increasingly clear to Calum. Ever since he first met her, she talked about the script for life as though it was a passing esoteric comment. He could never grasp exactly what she meant, being vague and coy when he sought more clarification. The script she so often alluded to, isn't a mere abstract concept; it is a narrative forming in her mind of their entangled hearts. The movie, intricately interwoven within their unfolding story, is what occupies her thoughts. As if by a magical force, their romance story is being artfully recreated in real life. She is looking for clues that would confirm the connection between them and the actors on screen, seeking assurance that it isn't a figment of her vivid imagination. Like her, now Calum can see their relationship from a totally different perspective, seeing it as a profound connection that defies the boundaries of an ordinary romance.

Calum: This feeling comes only for some fortunate people...it's always circumstances that get in the way of perfect union.

Halla: The scene where he stops the car and waits for her choice.

Calum: Very emotive.

Halla: They meet again on the bridge in Madison County in the distant future.

Calum: This movie is so sad. I am watching the end again now.

Halla: Look at their last choice.

Calum: They were together in the end...in spirit.

Halla: Every scene seems to pass by before my eyes.... after such a long time.

Calum: Oh My God, I was talking to you about a bathtub only a few days ago. There is a scene, you know the one. Is this movie about you and me, really?

Halla: Maybe. But so much more.

Calum: This is going to be a long winter without you.

Halla: *"In a universe of ambiguity...."*

Halla: There must be a reason why we met now. I am looking forward to what the story will be written for us.

Calum: We can be co-authors in the journey.

Halla: I know my inner passion thanks to you. I knew it was visible to others. You're shining light.

Calum: And some people are scared of the heat. Not me.

Halla: You are so funny. a scratching kangaroo.

Calum: I am going to watch it again. It has me fascinated.

Halla: This story is so beautiful because she chose her responsibility and he respected it.
Calum: Yes, lots to think about.
Halla: Enjoy. I will watch it with you at the same time even though you are far away.
Calum: I always said you were an artist. You have shown me something new. I can see this strange mystery between us and this movie. Thank you.

The film opens with Francesca, played by Meryl Streep, as she sends her family on a four-day excursion. Left alone on the farm, a stranger, Robert Kincade, Clint Eastwood, arrives asking for directions to a bridge he needs to photograph, as part of a National Geographic assignment.

Calum: That opening scene. That is like how we first got together at the river. I photographed the bridge!
Halla: Yes. I knew that soon after I met you.
Calum: I am looking at the photo I took of the bridge now. And the first thing, I offered you was a cigarette. What!

Their initial encounter, beside the Han River and the bridge that spans it, is like a page torn from the script of this classic love story. Calum, a retired photographer, discovers himself mirrored within the persona of Robert, portrayed by the enigmatic Clint Eastwood. It is as if the universe has conspired to align the writer's vision to influence the direction of Calum and Halla's life, their paths leading toward an inevitable connection in 3-dimensional reality.

Calum: This is a bit spooky for me. I don't know what to make of it.
Halla: Yes, it made me feel intrigued all the time we were together.

Calum: I understand now. When you were daydreaming, you were thinking about this movie.
Halla: Yes.

It is becoming apparent to both of them that perhaps, they are living out a script written by destiny itself. The realisation is confirmed for Halla. For Calum, it is new and unsettling.

Calum: I wish you would have told me when I was there. We could have watched it together.
Halla: We are watching it together ...just not side by side.

Francesca, a middle-aged lady, sees her life ebbing away in the boring, repetitive existence as a housewife, imprisoned by circumstance, on a remote farm. She had anticipated more from life. The sudden appearance of Robert is like an irresistible magnet that could take her away into a world of travel and adventure, a life she fantasized about frequently. She sees him as an opportunity and seduces him. Within a short time, it becomes a passionate affair, where they both fall in love.

Calum: Is this how you saw me? Someone who could take you away to another life.
Halla: I saw that it may be possible to escape my life with you, if I were to choose.
Calum: She seduced him, very much like you did with me. I didn't mind. I liked it.
Calum: I see you now in a completely different light.

Halla felt it prudent to remind Calum there were two people in the dance of seduction.

Halla: Yes, hungry lion. They both fell in love.
Calum: This line... do you remember we talked about; one plus one equalling one. It's so similar in meaning.

'We are hardly two separate people now', and,
'So here I am walking around with another person inside
of me.'
Calum: I remember you saying something like this at the
Karaoke bar on our first night out. 'And I am stalked now
by that other entity.'
Halla: Yes. I am so relieved you can see us in this movie.
I was worried.
Halla: I am happy you can see our relationship more
clearly. I said I would take you to Valhalla.

During the four days with Robert, Francesca bears the weight of
the responsibility of her children. Not unlike Halla, who struggles
with her devotion and commitment to her beloved cat and dog,
holding their interest well before her own. It is as though the tapestry of their own love story is intricately woven into the fabric of the
movie. Calum could see how their experience together is magnified
by this other mysterious element and how Halla identifies with the
circumstances of Francesca. Their relationship could well have been
scripted by the universe, where love and destiny weave together in
the most mysterious and enchanting way.

Calum: Will you make the same choice as Francesca,
choosing your pets over a life with me. Responsibility?
Halla: Calum! I don't have good stamina.
Calum: So many obstacles between us. Geographic,
language. Always circumstances that gets in the road
of perfect union.

Calum has to walk and think. As if there isn't enough to deal with
already without her being by his side. He wants to clear his mind,
but he then begins wrestling with the unexpected, the haunting
echoes of doubt. As the cold winter snow crunches under his feet, an

unsettling revelation dawns on him, that he might merely be a pawn in the elaborate tapestry of her theatrical world, an actor amidst the intricacies of her grand illusion.

> *Calum*: I am not sure what is real anymore. Are we those characters, or, are they us?
> *Halla*: Calum! the script has been written for us.

Chapter Twenty One

In Calum's mind, his view of their relationship is challenged as suspicion and logic intervenes.

He retraces his time with Halla, analysing some of the feelings he experienced, when she spoke of romance. He questions if her words were just dialogue, delivered by a character she plays opposite him in a rehearsed parallel universe. Calum's heart aches. These are questions he needs answers to, but how would he find the truth. Are her emotions genuine or merely a scripted performance, just props written by a writer, in another unknown distant land and time.

Halla: We cannot change the finish, the script...Kiss me. I don't like you. Ha.

That response felt like she is mocking him, he thought.

He is starting to suspect that she might be mapping the direction of their propinquity according to how the plot in the movie ends. She follows the script accurately, seducing him, pandering to his ego, showering him with affection and kindness. Praising him. Making him fall in love, feel loved. Does she even know what love is? Is it real? He begins to suspect, it isn't.

Calum: I am amazed and a bit uncomfortable with this whole thing.
Halla: The choices are sometimes made for us.

Calum begins to suspect he is dealing with a mad woman, or a master of shaping and manifesting reality. Everything is back the front. Rather than a real relationship evolving naturally, perhaps it is contrived and manipulated, and she, the one dictating the outcome all along. He can recognise there is a certain power in that.

"Wow," I have just been involved with an enchantress, a conjuror, he thought. Is she conscious of that power she has? Maybe, she doesn't even know it.

Yet, he recognises there were things outside of her control she is unable to manufacture and write into their relationship.

Calum: Even our personalities are similar. Robert said in the film that he loves everyone and no one in particular. That's what you said you liked about me.
Halla: Yes, you can talk to anyone as though they are your old friends. I like. Everywhere is your home.
Calum: I am interested in knowing if there are other similarities between us and the movie that you can see.
Halla: Yes. You are a writer and Robert was a journalist. I have your book. Robert sent Francesca his book. And you offered me a cigarette first day, just like in the movie.
Halla: And he gave Francesca blue flowers. I am holding your pendent with me now.

Calum cannot get the film, or her out of his mind. Just as he and the character, Robert, has much in common, he could see a similarity between Halla with her alter-ego, Francesca. But this too, seemed to be beyond anyone's ability and control, to replicate in real life.

Francesca Johnson sees her life and recognises it to be the limited extent of her unrealised potential. She yearns to be free of the prison she has built for herself and the circumstances of her existence. Along comes Robert Kincade. He is an opportunity to move beyond her comfort zone, a test for her to live out life being truly authentic. She needs the courage to break free of the demands of society and responsibility. The choice for her, is between the known and the unknown.

Halla is imprisoned by her own circumstance, in a similar way as Francesca. They both struggle and yearn to break free of self-imposed limitations. She has the responsibility of her cat and dog. But more than that, responsibility is a social pressure ingrained in the Korean psychology and culture; a duty imposed on her character from birth. Sacrifice is often depicted in popular Korean melodramas. What better way to lead an authentic Korean life, than to sacrifice love for responsibility. He had to be prepared for that possible outcome. It weighed upon her and he presumed it contributed to her ill-health. Like Francesca, she has the choice between the known and the unknown.

Francesca chose her familiar world, her responsibility to her children, as most mothers would. However, she then had to live out the rest of her life forever wondering how things might have been different, had she followed her heart. Calum questions if Halla can foresee that outcome for herself.

Calum predicted Halla will choose responsibility over a life with him, because to do otherwise, would mean a sense of personal failure, even though he believed she is accountable only to herself.

Calum delivered her a line straight from his ego.

Calum: Francesca saw Robert as erotic.
Halla: You are cute, cute, cute kangaroo.
Calum: Halla, Remember, I am coming back to Korea.

Do you think she made the right choice. What would you have done if you were Francesca?
Halla: It's very sad but I understand her. I would have done the same.

That gives him the answer he is suspecting might happen. She will most likely follow the script exactly. In the film, the actors eventually separated, never to see each other ever again.

Calum: If she had went to be with Robert, it would have been a difficult life. The same with us. I travel to underdeveloped countries. Living rough.
Calum: Can love overcome the difficulties of physical hardship?
Halla: I don't have good stamina.
Calum: I can deal with that. Halla, I need to confess, I started thinking you were the fallen goddess, Jacheongbi, when I was with you.
Halla: Are you crazy! But I like the comparison. Thank you.

Calum doesn't like her response. He felt it trivialised him. However, she brings up a question that demands an interrogation. Is he really crazy for thinking such a thing? Perhaps the answer is, yes, he thought.

Halla: My energy is all about work and taking care of my cat and dog. If something becomes more plus, my life patten is broken. I don't have good physical strength like before.
Halla: Everyone's life and love are already in another movie. Like our story.
Calum: The scene in the kitchen...it's almost the same as our last night in the hotel. The words.
Calum: You said to me once, the script is written already for us. What did you mean?

Calum: Halla! Are they 'walk ins' like the man that was chasing you?
Halla: Please understand. I am her. She is me.
You are him. He is you.
They are us. We are them.
Calum: Are they taking over our lives? Please can I call you?

Her silence spoke louder than words.

As is often the case in the grand complexity of love and life, there are hurdles to overcome. Distance, language, culture, responsibilities, cast long dark shadows across their path. Circumstances are actively foreshadowing the outcome of their future, just as the tide separates the moon from the sea, and a river, divides two land masses. What brought them together now threatens to tear them apart. The irresistible physical attraction that began the union of mind and body, that first ignited the erotic magnetism, transforms to become a mischievous troll under a bridge, conspiring to test the endurance of their affection and the strength of their love.

Halla: I am going to the hospital today.
Calum: Why, what is wrong?
Halla: I am itchy and it stings when I go to the toilet.
Calum: That's terrible!...I don't know what to say.
Halla: I am sure it's just that I am sensitive. I have to ask.
Do you have symptoms of STD. They will want to know.
Calum: No, I don't. If I did, you are the last person I would hurt.
Halla: I can feel your heart from the way you look at me, the way you act and speak. I know you are treating me with all your heart.
I wouldn't think you cheated on me if the cause of my problem was you.

Halla: I hope you don't feel distressed when you wake in the morning.

Halla: Calum! Do you remember the first time we met?

Calum: I remember a shining light near the river. The feeling of a profound connection in a taxi ride to the hotel. The angelic face looking down on me after you cooled me down with a wet towel in a hot hotel room.

I remember you with a cigarette lighter burning threads off my shorts. The funny Halla bouncing around the room, full of energy...talking, talking, talking and spilling beer. Singing and dancing.

The bright shiny eyes, the nice bum, the feeling of your arm in mine. You are imprinted on my memory for eternity, my friend.

Halla: I am getting tested for STD.

Calum: What time?

Halla: 1.pm. but it will take five days to get the results.

Calum: I am being totally honest. I have no symptoms.

Halla: People can be carriers but no symptoms. I have never had this before.

Calum: You are the last person I would want this to happen to. You are family to me. Of all the things, this is the worst.

Halla: We will see what the results are, not having had this before.

Now we wait. But they will ask me. Have you been with anyone and when?

Calum's world is rapidly coming undone around him. This is the worst possible thing to happen. How does a new relationship recover from this, already under stress from numerous angles, he wondered. Now is the time for the truth and it is forced. He hated himself. It felt dirty. "She will never forgive me if the results are STD," he said.

Calum: Three months ago ...in Cambodia.

There, it's out there. The truth. The hardest possible thing. He could lie, plead innocent, yet he is cornered. Check mate. There is no way out of this. She will hate me, he thought.

Halla: Cambodia is very dirty, like Thailand. You need to stop this promiscuity.

Calum felt like stating the obvious - stop picking up stray kangaroos in the park. He holds back on a rebuff, deciding to take it on the chin.

Calum: I am sorry this has happened. Absolutely devastated that I may have caused you any discomfort.
Halla: I believe you. We just have to wait.
Halla: It may be that I am sensitive. I have not had a relationship for 15 years.

Calum feels a weight lift, as he perceives there is forgiveness in her reply. This event didn't happen in the film. Who wrote this amendment to our script. It supposed to be happy ever after, he pondered.

But still, something isn't right. Calum's mind wrestles with an unsettling feeling that refuses to be quelled, unaccustomed as he is to having a similar disturbance of this nature in his life. A revelation claws at the edges of his consciousness. A disquiet begins to unfurl as his fingers trace the contours of the gift bag Halla had given him. He retrieves her accidently placed token of affection, the small vial of feminine lotion, a seemingly innocent balm used for a common itch. Calum's brow furrows with a realization. This, he surmises is not the first time Halla's has had the discomfort of an itch, although she said she has never experienced the symptoms before. The lotion, a silent witness to a recurring affliction, becomes a harbinger of suspicion with the possibility, he is the victim of deceit. Liars, he mused, were akin to thieves, leaving behind subtle traces of their misdeeds. The psychological need to be caught, a clandestine desire to be exposed, manifests in the subtle clues scattered along the pathway of deception.

Calum resolves to carry this evidence, although anecdotal, to the grave. The world of passion and intimacy is becoming a treacherous terrain, fraught with suspicion. The fragility of trust, disintegrating rapidly. Yet love, is an ever-present, clinging emotion, which he cannot shake.

The days tick away painfully slow until the results come.

Halla: I have the results. It is not STD. It's a bacteriuria infection like thrush.
Calum: I am so relieved and exhausted from the stress. I am so happy and so sorry that I may have caused you discomfort.
Halla: Oh! I make you tired! I have to take 10 antibiotics. Every day!

He is disturbed about this new information. "Ten antiviral tablets a day? He questions the truth of her text. Seems like an excessive exaggeration, he thought.

The great distance across the Pacific Ocean between Korea and Canada, a vast expanse of turbulent sea, becomes similar to the turmoil that is forming in their relationship. Calum is disturbed already by the revelation about her physical health. Now he is increasingly worried having learned she is taking antibiotics on top of anti-depressants and sleeping pills, a toxic mixture of mind-altering drugs. She is probably not eating properly either and drinking alcohol, he presumes. That is enough artificial chemicals to tip any sane person over the edge, affecting her entire physiological system causing rashes, itchiness and a multitude of other ailments.

Calum knows there are numerous forces at work that will tear them apart. Korea celebrates 'singles day' or Black day. The opposite to Valentine's Day, a Korean practice, gaining popularity where people who are without partners dress in black, celebrate their independence. He remembers Halla wore her best black dress on their last night out. Was she sending him a subliminal message, within a cloaked disguise? She has broken the Korean cultural rule, known as 369. No sex before three months into a new relationship, or six months, perhaps nine. He remembers 369 was the number written on the card the man gave him in the hotel foyer. He surmised it is a private reminder message to Halla, from her family.

He wonders if the 4B phenomena, a philosophy she embraces will influence her decision. Maybe she hates herself and him, for falling into the temptation of seduction, seeing him as a reminder of her own personal and cultural failure.

But, what can one do as the pathways of love intersect, when suddenly, a fork is impaled in the roadway. He feels as if Halla is beginning to write her own script without him in it, while he is writing his, which includes her. In many ways, they are like two opposing universes colliding and meeting at a place called love. But for them, the impact could mean total disintegration and separation.

Halla calls to her canine friend as she heads for the door. "Mongee. Sorry, I have to do this on my own." she said, the weight of determination hung in her voice, echoing the gravity of the task at hand. She passes by a used bottle of sleeping pills and several empty beer cans piled up neatly in the corner of the kitchen. They vibrate, as the door behind her slams shut.

Winter is falling across the Korean landscape where, once again she is walking beside the Han River. The Olympic bridge, symbolically lost to a distant heavy fog. What was once a favourite place to walk and breathe the cool river air, now it is a tainted mix of memories, some painful and disturbing, others intoxicatingly beautiful. She approaches the seat where Calum had sat. "This is the place where it began, therefore, it should also be where it ends," she whispers, as if the wind itself could carry her haunting words to the ghosts of the past.

Halla is in emotional turmoil. "I not need! I not need men!" She sits down with her mobile in readiness to write a text, anguish etched across her face. Leaves fall like tears from the nearby Ginkgo trees. Her dark intelligent eyes have lost their brightness. Images of Francesca's torment and Robert's bewilderment flood her mind along with her seductive erotic lovemaking with Calum.

Her mood is dark, somber and erratic. The seat where they met is cold to her touch, a reflection of the temperature of her heart. A lone Cinereous vulture flies high above her, gliding on the winter's wind. She has come here to sever the ties, thereby relinquishing the melancholy shadows of the past. The river flows on, a silent witness to the torturous catharsis unfolding on its banks.

> *Calum*: Do you think we have the power to write our own script for life? I think we can change destiny.
> *Calum*: I will be back in 105 days.

Within her ethereal, wild, artistic, mental landscape, Halla is transforming a romantic connection with Calum into a personal belief that transcends the ordinary notions of love. In her heart she believes it is not a mere happenstance, rather, a perfect creation, a manifestation of mystical intervention. With that, she clings to an unchangeable, self-imposed law; a cosmic force dictates, if their paths are to cross again in this life, they cannot be reunited in the afterlife. Like the ending of the movie, a poignant and bittersweet twist, a narrative woven from her intricately contorted fantastical story. But even within her contrived reality, she can't escape the emotional pain of what she is about to do.

"We must not," her voice stung the crisp Korean air, a declaration that resonates with the celestial beings who watch over her. "Never meet again."

This is a decree whispered to the cosmos from her soul, a sacred pact that adds a layer of complexity to their connection. It is her way of preserving the magic, the ethereal connection that binds them, the gravitational pull of love, an overwhelming force that draws her inexorably towards him and yet, pushes him away.

As if seeking reassurance, her gaze lingers on the clouds above where the goddess, Jacheongbi, presides. "He must never break the spell," she said, fearing a great unravelling of their eternal bond. "We never, never see each other again this life," she clarifies, as though the grand complexity of existence should hear. This is a declaration that resonates deep. This enchantment, she casts upon their shared destiny, is final.

Halla: 100 days. I will be old. Don't come looking for me!

Calum is disturbed by her total change in character. Her comment reminds him of what she said to him on the first day they met. The trust that has arrived ever so slowly, is now evaporating rapidly. But it gets worse. The descent into confusion and separation is like a giant ugly boulder gaining volume and menace as it rolls down after him. There is nowhere to run, nowhere to hide.

Halla: I hate you. I don't miss you.
Halla: And the last 4B is, No! No to heterosexual relationships altogether. That means you!

"He never come back after that. I have good excuse," she said. When she sends this next message, it will be the end of their relationship for sure, she thought. "I need to make sure." He won't like receiving this, she commiserated. "So final. It's so final. But I have to do this." Francesca would want her to do it. She did it in the film and Halla feels her pain and empathises with her anguish.

"I have responsibility." I have my dog and cat. You had your children. You chose responsibility over love. I must do the same.... to make everything right. I not change script. Her internal dialogue tears at her mind. "I cannot see him ever again!"

With her finger poised like a trigger, she cries out of the depths of her confusion, "Calum. Robert. Calum, Robert! I love you so much! Please forgive me. "It must be done.! See you in the end. Then you will understand. We will be together again, my kangaroo."

She presses the send button on her mobile phone as if it were a detonator, knowing the explosive effect will be felt on the other side of the world.

> *Halla*: I have to understand the damn Australian who
> only speak English.
> Grow up. Damn Australian. Congratulations!
> I recommend Japan to you!
> You hang out with Japan.
> Japanese people are just like you.
> Fuck you, Australian.

In the distance, a man of middle eastern appearance approaches Halla. He is flanked by two nurses. Further away, out of sight, Halla's mother, is beside herself with anxiety.

"She has always been a challenge since young. Always different, an artistic, dreamy type."

A painful decision is forced upon Halla's mother, to take action they hope will save her daughter's life. Her friend, Mr 7.30, is there beside her providing reassurance and support. In the back seat, sits a lady who Calum had conversed with in a cafe early in his relationship with Halla.

"It will be ok now. We have found her at last." the lady said to Halla's mother.

Calum cannot believe that this is his Halla. It doesn't sound like the lady he knows and loves. Something is not right. She is rapidly becoming a complete foreigner to him in every aspect. Her way of thinking, her tone, now her foul language is alien. He wonders if it is the toxic chemicals she is taking and if he made a mistake not contacting her family.

"What kind of person did I get involved with," he relented.

Halla is keeping true to the script, he thought. But he doesn't know how to respond. He takes pity on her realising she has numerous mental and personal issues to deal with. He also understands it takes more than love alone to deal with severe mental illness. He knows he is out of his depth.

His reply is measured, refusing to engage in a downward spiral of negative retort. This is what Robert would say to Francesca, because he loved her and this is also what Calum would say to Halla, because he loves her.

Calum: Such anger and fear!
I choose not to live that way.
The earth is not my battlefield
and people are not my enemies.
I cannot help you. I don't know how to help you and I'm
so sorry for that... and for you.

Calum tries everything to rekindle their communication back to the way it was when love was new.

Calum: Halla!!! Don't you realise we are supposed to be together. You cannot deny our connection. It's in our script. The universe has given us the evidence. Look at the magic of what has happened. Don't go this way. Come back to me!!!

That is the last he ever heard from her. Halla disappeared into the shadows of time and space. She has written the script for the final chapter of their relationship. But Calum has difficulty accepting the ending. This is how it should have finished, he thought; We should be together from the first moment we fell in love. From that time on, until forever. True love never finishes, he thought.

However, Halla knows a painful truth - a beautiful romance, invariably involves separation.

It hurt. Calum felt manipulated, tricked, discarded and powerless. His understanding is, he is nothing more to her than a fictional character in her illusion. To him, the entire love affair, a complete fabrication and his Halla, a convincing actress. Not unlike the actor from Raiders of the Lost Ark, Calum doesn't want his part in her movie to end. Unresolved questions sweep over him. He lives with the difficulty of these emotions, constantly tearing at his heart.

Years later, as old age stalks the hungry lion, in moments of quiet solitude, his mind wanders back to those beautiful days beside the Han River, in the Land of the Morning Calm. He is mentally exhausted by the continual struggle to understand the encounter with her, in all its complexity. He lives the life of a lone wolf, free of the entanglements of relationships.

Unbeknown to him, Halla's concentrated love formula has a built-in delayed reaction designed to open his mind and which eventually brings him to a revelation. A soft breeze carries a profound understanding. The love he feels for her, the concern for her welfare, if he can transpose those same intense feelings to all people, there would be no feelings of loss or regret.

"Feel, don't think," he said. Just remember the feeling. Forget about things said that were wrong and hurtful, words of anger or fear, he thought. Just concentrate on the feeling he has, the feeling of love. With that, came some peace of mind.

In that exact same second, a text arrived. At first, he thought it is unsolicited mail. Upon closer examination, he sees it is an article from an online platform that reports on technology and scientific phenomenon. It reads:

Astronomers find a planet, named Halla, that shouldn't exist.

The planet Halla was first discovered by a team of Korean astronomers. They used the radial velocity method. This technique observes the movement of a star caused by the gravitational....

"That's her!!! That's my Halla! She did it. She promised to be a fire in the sky." Now he knows where to find her, his bright and shining light. "Gamsahamnida. Salanghaeyo," he shouts. In his excitement, he knocks over a cup of sedatives his nurse has prepared for him. Molly scrambles for cover.

"Calum! Be careful," said the nurse.

"Not Calum! My name is Robert. Robert Kincade."

Calum knows theirs is a complete and perfect romance in so many ways. Eventually, he understands, that practicing unconditional love for all sentient beings completes the circle of life.

Beside the Han River, in the Hanan suburb just a few kilometres away from Olympic Park in Seoul, South Korea, there stands an unremarkable park bench. Its design doesn't boast any extraordinary features, yet, an air of mystery and magic envelops it with an invisible embrace.

This unassuming seat, holds a secret promise for those who seek love, intimacy, or an unforgettable connection. It whispers tales of perfect unions, memorable and intense.

To those who yearn for the tender touch of love, you are invited. It can be found at the end of Pungseong-ro street after entering through a long dark tunnel towards the river. It resonates with the promise of serendipitous encounters, mysterious and profound. Rest assured; it will weave its spell when least expected. If its love you seek, then you should go.

However, as the river's current carries the promise of connection, there is a question lingering in the air—will the story which unfolds, be the one you hope for? Is the love that arrives, be what you dreamed of. Or perhaps, destiny has a different script for you?

The bench waits, with tales of enchantment, alure, of hearts entwined, longing and lust...or perhaps loss.

Yes, you should go.

Lindsay McAuley grew up living close to nature on a sheep and cattle station in outback Queensland, Australia. This is where he first acquired an interest in astronomy, art and metaphysics.

A career in the film industry and photography helped develop creative skills. As an extension to his artistic nature, he obtained a certificate in art and went on to win awards as a visual artist and in film making.

A prolific creator, his talents are diverse.

He has written several plays and now, an author, having completed a book entitled, *The Lost World of the Maya*. This research challenges and expands history's understanding of the Maya civilisation. *Scent of a Lion*, is his first novel set in South Korea. Also in development, is a children's educational book, The Adventures of Kanga, the Lost Kangaroo, based in Cambodia. He has written research reports on subjects as diverse as anatomy, astronomy and mathematics.

Lindsay's artwork has featured in several group and solo art exhibitions, including a fine-art photography exhibition entitled Skyharp. This project documents the changing light of the natural environment and its effect on an outdoor metallic sculpture which aligned with the equinox and the solstice.

Combining this varied background with an artistic sensibility and influenced by a social conscience, compelled him to undertake a project involving world peace and disarmament. Entitled, A 'Peace of Metal,' the concept involves participation of all the member states of the United Nations.

Restless by nature, Lindsay has travelled to 43 countries across all seven continents of the world.

www.lindsaymcauley.com